10-25-00
23.95

Jacqueline

*Also by Angela Gordon
in Large Print:*

A Game Called Love
Love in Her Life
Love Is a Tempest
Stranger in the Shadows

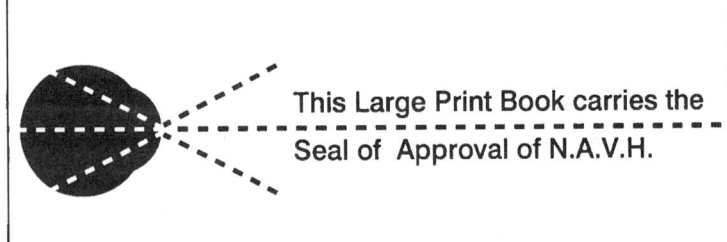

Jacqueline

Angela Gordon

G.K. Hall & Co. • Thorndike, Maine

© Robert Hale Limited 1970 and 1982

All rights reserved.

Published in 2000 by arrangement with Golden West Literary Agency

G.K. Hall Large Print Paperback Series.

The text of this Large Print edition is unabridged.
Other aspects of the book may vary from the original edition.

Set in 16 pt. Plantin by Christina S. Huff.

Printed in the United States on permanent paper.

Library of Congress Cataloging-in-Publication Data

Gordon, Angela, 1916–
   Jacqueline / by Angela Gordon
     p. cm.
   ISBN 0-7838-9180-6 (lg. print : sc : alk. paper)
   1.Triangles (Interpersonal relations) — Fiction.   2. Gardeners — Fiction. 3. Large type books. I. Title.
PS3566.A34 J3   2000
813´.54—dc21   00-057235

CONTENTS

1	The Spencer Men	7
2	The Spencer Estate	15
3	The Stranger	25
4	The Man in Dark Glasses	34
5	The Gardener and the Lady	43
6	A Talk by Starlight	52
7	To the City and Back	61
8	A Conspiracy	71
9	A Shocker	81
10	A Wet Night	91
11	A Curious Day	100
12	An Eavesdropper	109
13	Jacqueline	119
14	An End to Secrecy	129
15	After the Downpour	139
16	'I Love You!'	148
17	An Argument	157
18	A Moonlight Walk	167
19	The Long Wait	177
20	The Pay-Off	187
21	The Quiet Aftermath	197
22	A Happy Ending	207

Chapter One

THE SPENCER MEN

'What kind of a person has to be stared at,' growled Merritt Spencer, who was the widowed grandfather of the woman he was talking about. 'Granted little children do that to be noticed, or people with some variety of mental disturbance have to jump up and say. "Look at me, how wonderful I am", but good heavens, Harold, not Jacqueline, not your own daughter. She's making a spectacle of herself. It's disgusting.'

The younger man, also fair and blue-eyed, wide-shouldered and handsome in an aquiline, rather long-faced way, smiled. He looked a very healthy forty-five, while the older man, his father, looked a very craggy, rough and resourceful sixty-five. The men of clan Spencer almost invariably looked their real age. It was, however, something of a saving grace that they were also always honest, forthright, really very earthy and predictable men, in spite of wealth, and that was not very easy, normally, but the Spencers had been getting born to wealth for over two hundred years which made it much easier to accept and live with.

It also happened to be what was presently

annoying Merritt Spencer so much. 'Good heavens, Harold, it can't be the money she gets for that vulgar display she makes on the stage, so it's got to be that Jacqueline is an exhibitionist.' Merritt looked over at his son from where they were both sitting in shade upon the Grecian-style loggia of the older man's home. 'Are you aware, Harold, that exhibitionism goes hand in hand with immaturity? The girl is immature emotionally. It's never happened in the family before.'

'There is an old book upstairs in the study,' said Harold, knocking ice cubes against the walls of the glass he held upraised, 'that mentions one Bedelia Spencer, daughter of a Franklin Spencer of Lamb's Continental Artillery Corps of Washington's army, who set all Philadelphia agog with an affair she had with Aaron Burr, the gentleman who —'

'I know what he did, damn it, Harold. He killed Alexander Hamilton in a silly duel. All right. As for Bedelia — I think she was adopted.'

Harold broke out into soft laughter, and old Merritt turned blue, twinkling eyes, to watch. There was one more unique thing about the Spencer men; invariably they possessed a sense of humour. Even in dark hours, they were not unknown to make some drily or scandalously inappropriate remark, that either shocked or convulsed people. Often, though, that Spencer wit could be double-edged, as now, when Merritt said, 'Harold, I was driven to the city last evening and — took in, as they say — Jacqueline's act. She can't act. She is indeed adequately and voluptuously endowed. On the other hand she can't act. In fact I'm not sure she is even supposed to act. And neither can she dance. That leaves what I've just mentioned— exhibitionism. Now no matter where she inherited it, son, it must stop. This exhibitionism, I mean.'

Harold finished the drink, leaned to put the glass aside, settled back and admired the greenery beyond the marble balustrade of his father's loggia. 'Dad, Jacqueline is twenty-three years old.'

'Time she was married, then.'

'Perhaps,' conceded her father mildly. 'But the point is, she *isn't* married, and she *is* of the legal age of consent. I can't forbid her to go on with this acting career of hers . . . and you are quite right, she is a lousy actress. Also in that other respect, you are also correct: She is stacked.'

'She is what?'

'Extremely well built, Dad. Come join the rest of us in the twentieth century.'

'Humph!'

'Incidentally, I did that little favour for you. I brought out a new groundsman for you. He'll be round back with Domingo at the stable.'

'Good. Just once I'd like to get one that would stay. What are his recommendations?'

'He has none.'

'Confound it, Harold, I specifically told you, with all the silver and other junk around here I wanted a man who —'

'He was a paratroop officer in Europe and Asia, a mercenary in Israel, and a hired blockade runner on the West German autobahn.'

Merritt's craggy face curled into an odd expression. 'Well, what in the devil is he doing here as a yardman, then; hiding from someone — the Mafia, perhaps or . . . Harold, take him back with you. He can't possibly know anything about flowers and trees.'

'I can't take him back. Just to induce him to come out with me this morning I had to advance him one month's salary.'

Merritt was round-eyed with astonishment. 'One month in advance to induce him . . . ? What inducement; what kind of a damned fool stunt have you gone and done now? Why should you want to induce him, let alone advance his salary when I'm his employer, not you. And just what — ?'

'Dad,' said Harold, sliding down slightly in his chair, letting his head loll along the back of the chair so he could look upwards at the spotless blue sky, 'you need this man. It's not good for you, living out here like an old aloof hermit in the middle of a hundred acres of parkland with only a great mausoleum of a mansion and a couple of servants to keep you occupied.'

Merritt's colour mounted. 'You confounded busybody,' he snarled. 'Who are you — who can't even control your own daughter — to be sticking your big hooked nose into my affairs?

You always were an obnoxious child, Harold. And you take this cut-throat mercenary dog-robber back with you. As a matter of fact you can leave right now. Old aloof hermit . . . aloof, perhaps. It's my right if I choose to be aloof. And if I desire privacy I can have it. But old — why of all the insulting whelps . . . of all the ingrates . . . you are unquestionably the worst!'

Harold continued relaxed, head tilted, eyes watching the spun-glass pale haze drifting past overhead; it was as though the older man's angry tirade hadn't erupted. Then Harold said, 'There is one thing, though. I actually like the name.'

'I don't care what his name is. You can —'

'Not his name. *Her* name. I wish we'd actually named her Francesca.'

Merritt's steam ran out, but his manner did not alter as he said, with icy calm, 'Jacqueline was your grandmother's name. Francesca indeed; it sounds gypsyish. Anyway, foreign. Maybe even French, of all things.'

'Spanish.'

'What's the confounded difference: Spanish, French, Gypsy. All the same. In any case I'm glad she had the decency not to use her great-grandmother's name. Or perhaps it wasn't decency — she just couldn't recall that it was a family name.' Merritt tilted back his head, drained the highball glass, put it atop a little wrought-iron table with an inlaid tile top, and fished out a handkerchief to wipe both palms with.

It was quite warm even though where they sat was on the east side of the manor-house, with shade stretching away in front of them over the grass as far as the nearest hoary oaks.

Merritt's recent anger did not help much either, and although it seemed gone for now, actually only the first wave of it was gone. There was another unique thing about the Spencer men; they were fiercely stubborn about things they could not excuse. Fortunately they were also a tolerant lot, as a rule, so temper-tantrums such as old Merritt had just displayed were infrequent.

'She used to love coming out here and riding the horses,' said Harold. 'Exactly as I used to love it when I was a child.'

'You were never a genuine child, Harold. You were simply a very young old man. You were always dangerous. I told your mother more than once that if I'd read a book on eugenics when we'd first got married, damned if I'd have had any children.'

'Only one,' smiled Harold, watching his father's long, ruddy, lined face with its hawkish, high-bridged nose, turn dour and tough.

'More than enough, confound you.'

Harold laughed, shot upright in the chair and glanced at his wafer-thin gold wristwatch. 'It's getting on,' he said, but without moving.

'Yes. And take that brigand with you, too.'

'Can't. I told you. He's been paid in advance.'

'Well; take it back.'

Harold stood up, smoothed his jacket and said, 'Dad; go look at Mister Nufall. I'd rather he'd just keep the money.'

Merritt shot forward to arise. 'Nufall? Is that this thug's name?'

'No, Dad. His name is Neunteufel. Frederick Neunteufel. But he doesn't use that name.'

'Good Lord I don't blame him. How can anyone ever pronounce it, let alone spell it? Nufall is some improvement, but not much.'

'It's not that, Dad,' stated Harold quietly. 'You see, in German the same name means nine devils.'

'Nine . . . ? Harold, you have a very perverted sense of humour.'

'Dad, this is the absolute truth. He told me when he was younger every now and then someone who spoke German would make a big issue, there would usually be a fight, so he changed it to Nufall. Kept his first name, which is Fred, but changed the other name.'

Merritt heaved himself up out of the chair with a mild curse and a great sigh, put a dolorous stare upon his son and said nothing for as long as it required him to push both hands deep into trouser pockets and stroll to the edge of the marble-walled and marble-paved loggia. There, with his back to his son he said, 'The object of my asking you to come out here, was to discuss your daughter. But it has never failed, Harold; when we talk seriously something else is always brought up, and nothing is ever settled between us.'

'Dad, you said for me to find someone and bring him —'

'A man named nine devils?' roared the older man, whirling. 'Some damned pirate you found in a gin-mill? Harold; you go find that man, then the pair of you get the hell out of here and don't come back until — God forbid! — I send for you again!'

'Dad, listen for just a —'

'*Go.* Confound you, get out of my sight. Find Mister Nine Confounded Devils and go!'

Merritt drew himself up ramrod-erect, glared, then stamped past his son and slammed the French doors that gave egress to the marble loggia.

Harold gazed briefly at the glass door, then raised and dropped his shoulders, went out to his car, climbed in, punched the starter and without a backward glance started down the long, curving macadamed drive that led beyond a high iron fence, past two sentinel stone towers where the electrically-operated gates were, and cut left when he reached the main thoroughfare, heading back for the city.

Chapter Two

THE SPENCER ESTATE

At one time Merritt Spencer had maintained a staff for the manor-house, but a number of years earlier he had closed the entire upper section, had moved to the first floor, and had also curtailed much of his former social and business activity, with the result that he now lived in the manor-house with just one indoor servant, a sturdy woman of forty or forty-five whose reddish hair, pale-blue eyes and shoebutton nose might have given a hint of her origin even if her name were not Erin Patricia Clancy.

At one time, too, Merritt Spencer had shown horses, as a hobby, and had ridden in a number of hunts — one as far away from Chicago's environs as Kentucky, another in Virginia. But after the passing of his wife years earlier, he had also given that up. He kept several horses in the delightful stone-and-log barn out beyond his manor-house garden, and occasionally went forth to exercise an animal, but those periods had been getting fewer and farther between for some time now.

His stableman was a swarthy, barrel-shaped, grinning man named Domingo Salazar, a durable and cheerful individual of Mexican descent.

It was Domingo, rolling one of his little brown-paper cigarettes out front of the stable that evening after Harold had driven back to Chicago, that Merritt encountered as he went striding forth in search of Frederick Nufall.

Domingo's dark face split into a mahogany grin at sight of his employer. He lit the little cigarette and hitched up his sagging trousers, something he did almost unconsciously whenever Mister Spencer appeared. There was a good relationship between those two, employer and employee, exactly as there was between Erin Clancy and her employer. Perhaps Harold, who lived in the tumult of urban Chicago, thought his father was vegetating out on the estate, but it was less a matter of vegetation than it was a matter of old fashioned values and virtues on the one hand, and the breezy sophistication of a younger man on the other hand.

Merritt cast a slow glance roundabout, found the stables immaculate as they always were, then sidled closer to the blanket-rack where Domingo was leaning and said,

'Where is that man my son brought out today?'

Domingo turned slightly and jutted with his chin towards the cottage-like living quarters at the far end of the stable-building. 'I gave him the vacant room at the end,' he said quietly, with only a bare trace of accent. 'He is getting settled.' Domingo's jet-black eyes turned back and lifted.

'He is going to make a very good man, Mister Spencer.'

'Is he now? Well, I don't intend —'

'He fixed Mrs. Clancy's car in fifteen minutes, and you know it hasn't run for two months.'

'He did that?'

'Yes sir. And he splinted that Chinese Elm tree that the wind broke. He is very clever about such things, Mister Spencer. I think your son found us a very good man. Of course, they don't usually stay, do they?' Domingo smiled over this and shrugged his shoulders in a purely Latin manner, implying that something was unfortunately preordained.

'This one wouldn't in any case,' Merritt answered, gazing thoughtfully down where a light had just come on behind a curtained window down at the far end of the stable-building.

Domingo said, 'Maybe you are right, but my own feeling is that this is the one that *will* stay.'

Merritt dropped his gaze. 'Oh?'

'I think so. He doesn't like cities. He told me that. And he likes doing things with his hands. Well; there is plenty to do around here with one's hands. Always something . . .'

Merritt sidled a little closer and lowered his voice. 'Tell me, Domingo, has he said anything about himself?'

'Well; only that he was once a soldier, and that he has travelled quite a bit.' Domingo spread his hands. 'He has only been here this afternoon.' The cheerful smile came up. 'Mrs. Clancy liked him.'

'Did she?' said Merritt. 'How do you know that?'

'She talked with him for a bit, then asked if he liked corned beef and cabbage for supper.'

Merritt nodded his head, convinced. Erin Clancy had a way of letting them all know, including her employer, when she was displeased. She'd been with Merritt Spencer seven years, not as long as Domingo Salazar had been with him, but long enough to know the favourite dish of each one of them. When they displeased her she served only things they did not much care for. It was indeed a feather in the new man's cap if she had offered to make corned beef and cabbage for supper. It was one of her specialities. No one, to Merritt Spencer's way of thinking, could cook it as well as she could.

Domingo studied his employer, the straight, downward lashes shielding his black eyes. He was smiling still, but shrewdly now. He too had been with Mister Spencer long enough to understand certain things. For instance, he had guessed just from the way Mister Spencer had approached him that Mister Spencer had not come to offer a welcome to the new man.

But Domingo was convinced Fred Nufall was exactly what they needed on the estate. More important, he had a feeling that *this* newcomer would stay, and that was important because Domingo not only did not like doing the yardwork, he wasn't very good at it. So now he said, 'You know, Mister Spencer, I am getting too old for the yardwork and stable work too. Maybe if you could find a younger man . . .'

They regarded each other steadily, and gradually it dawned upon Merritt Spencer what was happening. He was not a man to bow to any intimidation, but this was different. Domingo was as much a part of the estate as the horses, or the grounds, or even the manor-house itself. He stood watching Domingo smoke his brown-paper cigarette, then he said very softly, 'Well, maybe this man will work out, Domingo. You can show him around.'

The broad smile returned. 'I will be glad to.' Domingo dropped the cigarette and very carefully ground it to pieces underfoot. 'You will like him. Maybe we should go down there right now so you can meet him.'

'No,' said Merritt. 'It's almost dinner time. I'll look him up in a day or two.' Merritt straightened up. 'How are the horses?'

'Fine, Mister Spencer. If you wished to exercise one . . . ?'

'In a day or two, maybe. I've got something else on my mind.'

'Yes. I know. Your granddaughter.'

Merritt perhaps should have been surprised, but after so many years with these people he also knew something; by some mysterious means of communication both Domingo and Erin Clancy always knew exactly what was happening in his life.

That used to annoy him; he was a person who not only valued his privacy but also valued his personal aloofness. On the other hand, since neither Erin nor Domingo were the kind of servants who offered admonitions or unsolicited advice — were in fact intensely loyal and sympathetic — he had long ago become resigned. In fact, now and then when he needed someone to sound out ideas upon, he would use whichever of them was handiest, as now, when he said, 'It's a disgrace, that's what it is, my own granddaughter making a spectacle of herself. It shames the whole family.'

Domingo leaned upon the sturdy pole at his back, which was usually used only for draping wet horse-blankets to dry after washing, and considered the distant lighted back of the house as he said, 'People are different from how they were when I was a young man.'

That was neither a very profound nor novel pronouncement. Merritt said, 'Decency has always been decency. It's a disgrace, what Jacqueline is doing.'

'My sister had a daughter,' stated the stableman. 'Once they reach a certain age what can a parent do? Nothing. Because it has all been done by then. Either the parent sees the fruits of her work, or she sees the failure of it.'

That was not particularly profound either, but it held Merritt's attention briefly, before he finally said, 'Yes indeed. That confounded son of mine was remiss.'

'He is a widower,' murmured Domingo Salazar, preferring that word to the one Merritt said.

'Divorced, you mean.'

'Anyway, the girl grew up without a mother.'

'Yes.'

Domingo began to build another of those little brown-paper cigarettes. It was getting late, the sun had been gone several hours and although it remained quite warm, there were great shadows over everything.

'What can you do, Mister Spencer? Once a child becomes an adult, what can anyone do? With my sister's girl — she went away to California with a young man. It broke my sister's heart, but what could she do?'

Merritt Spencer wasn't thinking of Domingo's sister. 'Harold will do nothing,' he muttered. 'I'm sure of that. Not that I was very hopeful when I had him drive out today. But he's one of those permissive people, which is exactly why the girl is making this spectacle of herself. Unless she's some kind of exhibitionist; some kind of limited mentality.'

'I don't think she is like that,' said Domingo, lighting his fragrant little cigarette. 'She used to ride out here. She was very bright, quick to learn, good about listening when she was told something. No, Mister Spencer, your granddaughter — maybe she is an artist.'

It was the wrong thing to say. Merritt turned and glowered. 'Domingo, I can tell you unequivocally that she is *not* an artist. She dances poorly, can't act at all, and has only one reason for being up there on that stage at all — pulchritude. It's degrading and degenerate!'

Domingo retreated easily. 'It must be as you say, Mister Spencer.'

Over at the house a bell rang. That was the signal for the outside help to wash up and head for the huge kitchen, where Erin Clancy fed them. Inside the house, she was less strident and hunted up Mister Spencer to announce dinner in the dining-room.

He left Domingo and went strolling back the way he had come. He had not accomplished what had been his objective when he'd gone out to the stable, but he wasn't really very concerned about that. Domingo had started him thinking of his granddaughter again. All his reflections for the balance of the evening would be coloured bleakly by this.

Perhaps that was the worst feature about living alone in a private world; one concentrated too much, tended to brood, to compare things as they once were with how they now were, and become soured.

Erin Clancy met Mister Spencer when he entered the house and told him his dinner would be served in a few minutes. He nodded and started on past, to go to wash, but she stopped him with what else she said.

'Your son called from the city, Mister Spencer. He asked me to tell you that he would be driving out tomorrow with his daughter and her fiancé.'

'Her fiancé?' exclaimed Merritt. 'I had no idea

that she had one.' He slowly worked up a smile. 'What a relief, Erin. What a wonderful relief. Now she'll settle down.'

Mrs. Clancy barely inclined her head in a nod, and she did not smile as though to share her employer's sudden sense of relief and pleasure. Merritt noticed that, stood watching a moment, then lost his own smile as he gruffly said, 'Well, out with it, woman, out with it.'

'I have nothing more to report, sir.'

'Haven't you? Mrs. Clancy let me remind you that between you and Domingo Salazar whatever is going to happen around here, one or both of you know about it before it occurs. Now then, with some reason to feel pleased that my granddaughter has finally decided to act mature — there you stand looking as though the world shall end tonight at the stroke of midnight. Now out with it, woman; what is wrong?'

'Sir, your son simply said he and your granddaughter would be along, bringing her fiancé.'

'There was more to it than that, woman.'

'One other thing, Mister Spencer. The name of the fiancé.'

'For heaven's sake, Mrs. Clancy, do I have to drag it out of you a syllable at a time?'

'No sir. The man's name is Nick Esparza.'

For a moment they stood looking at one another. It took that long for Merritt Spencer to make anything out of that name. Not that he did not subscribe to the newspapers, hadn't perhaps heard the name in Chicago newscasts, but he had never had any contact with the underworld in his social nor business life, so he had to think a bit to link the name with Mrs. Clancy's flinty and disapproving expression.

'The hoodlum, Mrs. Clancy?' he eventually murmured.

'I don't know any other Nick Esparza, Mister Spencer.'

'I see. Did my son say it was the hoodlum?'

'No sir. Your son didn't say anything at all, except the name.' Mrs. Clancy struggled to brighten her expression. 'Of course you may be exactly right, sir. It may not be *that* Nick Esparza at all. Well, sir, supper is ready.' Mrs. Clancy turned and marched back to her kitchen.

Chapter Three

THE STRANGER

It was not as far-fetched as it seemed, but Merritt Spencer had to light a pipe and go strolling the front garden in the warm to believe it.

What encouraged his conviction was the fact that his granddaughter had evinced some kind of abnormal tendencies. Otherwise he never for a moment would have thought her fiancé could be *that* Nick Esparza.

He thought about returning to his study to telephone Jay Logan, his attorney. Logan also happened to be one of the most outstanding defence lawyers in the country, although his speciality was estate and corporate law.

If anyone would know the *real* Nick Esparza story, it would be Jay.

But in the end Merritt did not return to the house. It was a beautiful night, and being a respectable distance from the city, the sky was clear, the air fresh, the silence deep and enduring.

He went across to a stone bench near some aspen trees and sat, enjoying his pipe and trying to rationalize himself out of his granddaughter's life. If she chose to make a spectacle of herself, it was unlikely he could do anything about it, and since Harold obviously didn't much care, or at least acted as though he didn't, and *he* was her *father,* the situation was probably quite *hopeless.*

But he had adored Jacqueline as a child. Even as a girl with her hair flying, riding a horse around the estate bareback, he'd thought she was rather special.

Of course, as she'd budded into a young woman, he hadn't seen her as much. In fact he hadn't seen her for about half a year now; not since last Christmas when, traditionally, his son and his son's family came out to the estate for the holidays.

At that time he hadn't known she was on the stage. He *had* noticed some changes though; beautiful though Jacqueline was, she had been doing things to her hair, her eyes, her cheeks, to enhance it. The result had been something sleek, expensive, very sophisticated.

He hadn't cared much for what she'd smilingly called her 'new image', but kept that to himself.

And now this bum. This Nick Esparza, notorious as a playboy, a racketeer of some kind, a man whose name had been linked with dozens of those Reno-type females. A man of questionable background who had made a fortune in dubious ways, who was cocky, rude, and smilingly contemptuous of the things Merritt Spencer held to be the proper standards.

There was more, Merritt was positive of that,

but without talking to his attorney he had no idea how much more. He didn't really care, right at the moment. What he could recall reading about Esparza in the newspapers was enough.

But strictly speaking, Jacqueline's life was her own to live — and ruin — as she saw fit.

He leaned to knock the pipe empty against the stone bench and say aloud, 'Be damned if it is. There's the matter of the name. The entire family has seen to it that the name meant something among decent people. Be damned if she should be allowed to do *this* to it!'

A heavy silhouette moved silently across the grass not a hundred feet from where Merritt sat. He looked up, startled, watched the man stroll onward, and guessed the stranger would have to be the man Harold had brought out from the city.

Before speaking, Merritt made a study of the man. He was about six feet tall, graceful, moved with easy stride of a muscular individual, and his shoulders cut a wide, dark shadow in the night.

Merritt said, 'Hello there,' and watched the man turn smoothly in mid-stride the way an athlete might do, but not the way an ordinary, sedentary person would be able to do.

'Over here, over at the stone bench.'

The shadow hesitated only for a second, then strolled over. Up close, even in the starlight, Merritt could see the man's wide, curving mouth, the thrust of his square jaw, and the shadowed set of well-spaced light eyes.

Merritt stood up and shoved out a hand. 'You'll be Frederick Nufall,' he said. 'I'm Merritt Spencer.'

The man's grip was gentle but with a restrained powerfulness to it. He nodded without speaking, and continued to examine his employer.

Merritt, feeling the difference between them, said, 'Beautiful night. From now on we should have some dandies. It's a shame people sit indoors on evenings like this, watching anything as fatuous as television.'

The muscular man nodded, smiled slightly and answered. 'No accounting for people's tastes, Mister Spencer.'

Merritt shot him a quick look. There seemed to be something behind that quiet statement. Perhaps the man had been visiting with Domingo, had already heard a few things about the Spencers.

Merritt sat back down, looked around, then said, 'Well; from what you've seen so far, Mister Nufall, what do you think of the place?'

'It's very peaceful, Mister Spencer.'

'Well, what I was wondering about was whether you felt capable of taking over the maintenance of the grounds. Domingo hates working with flowers and bushes. He's never told me that, but then he doesn't have to; all I've got to do is look around.'

'I can do the work,' said Nufall. 'Regardless of my lack of references in this line, horticulture has been a hobby of mine for years.'

'Odd hobby for a professional soldier, Mister Nufall.'

'Not really, Mister Spencer. You were a very successful businessman, but you kept this estate. I think most active people have two sides to them. Maybe one compensates for the other.'

That was well said. Merritt studied his new employee with fresh interest. He was usually a blunt man, so now he said, 'You appear to have several side-interests. Making old cars run, splinting trees, wishing to be alone — at least I assume the last is your reason for coming here.'

'You assume correctly,' smiled Nufall, still standing in front of Spencer. 'As for Mrs. Clancy's car and the tree — using the hands is pretty good therapy.'

'I see. Of course I agree with you. Only now I'm wondering — do you need therapy, Mister Nufall?'

The man laughed softly. 'Not the way you mean. I just happen to know, that for me at least, working with the hands, getting away from the world where everyone is trying their damnedest to suck the blood from everyone else, is pleasant. But I'm not suffering from any hangups.'

'Hangups?'

'Psychotic difficulties, Mister Spencer. Bruised inhibitions.'

'Oh, I see. Well, that's very interesting. Would you care to sit? There's plenty of room, it's a large bench.'

'Standing is just fine.'

Merritt looked at the cold pipe in his hand. 'You've had a bull-session with Domingo, I assume.'

'We've talked.'

'I can imagine,' murmured Merritt drily. 'Between my housekeeper and stableman, I don't have any secrets. The point is, Mister Nufall, what did Domingo tell you about my — hangups?'

'Not very much, sir. We discussed the estate. The horses, the gardens, the things I'll have to do around here.'

'And my son and granddaughter, no doubt.'

Nufall stood silent, his gaze lingering upon the older man. He was not going to volunteer any more, obviously.

Merritt nodded slightly. 'It's all right. If I had been going to fly into a rage about what those two said concerning my affairs, believe me it would have happened long ago. Tell me something, Mister Nufall: Have you ever heard of a man named Nick Esparza?'

'Only what I've read in the newspapers.'

'Well; he is my granddaughter's fiancé. What do you think of that?'

'What should I think of it, Mister Spencer? It's none of my business. But if your granddaughter likes Nick Esparza, she must have her reasons.'

'But the man is a fortune-hunter, a scoundrel, a moral cripple, and if that isn't enough . . .' Merritt blew out a ragged sigh, and didn't finish the sentence.

Nufall nodded as though in agreement with everything his employer had said. But his next comment was in the same vein as what he'd said before. 'You and I don't have to look at him or be around him. Maybe your granddaughter sees something in him we wouldn't see. Anyway, it's her affair, isn't it?'

Merritt raised his eyes. 'Is it? Someone has to be concerned about other things, Mister Nufall — like the family name, and the girl's future happiness.' Merritt suddenly dropped the pipe into a jacket pocket and growled a mild curse. 'My son, Mister Nufall, has had everything handed to him on a silver platter, the best schools, trips round the world, wealth, comfort, and finally, ruling status of a multi-million dollar business enterprise that nearly runs itself. Do you know what I think?'

'No sir.'

'I think indulgent parents are at the root of two-thirds of the evil in this damned world. Harold was our only child. He was the apple of my wife's eye — and she was my only hobby — my only love — and after she died every time I'd get angry at my son, I'd see her looking at me with that expression of reproach she used to use when I'd discipline Harold. So — I just kept overlooking things until it was too late. And now Harold is acting the same way towards Jacqueline. He gave her everything — he ruined her — and now look what it's come to. She's going to marry a man like this Esparza.'

Fred Nufall stood silently watching the older

man. His features were strong, hard, even handsome in a very masculine way, and the dark blue eyes appeared to have an ability to look deep inside a man like Merritt Spencer.

Finally, the older man rose, glanced around, looked up at the endless sky, then dropped his head and said, 'Hell of a note. First day on the job and already you've had to assume the role of Father Confessor. You know, this kind of familiarity is what the man meant when he said it breeds contempt. Well; there's no denying that I almost share your opinion of me. The rich man who failed where it really mattered.'

'Aren't you settling for surrender before anyone has pointed a gun at you, Mister Spencer?'

Merritt thought that over. 'Possibly. But when you reach sixty, Mister Nufall, you are going to make a discovery: The world has rushed past and somewhere along the line you've been left behind. It becomes much easier to *see* what is wrong than it is to do anything about it.'

Nufall smiled softly in the shadows. 'Maybe. But age isn't your years, it's your mental attitude.'

Merritt thought about that too, and slowly examined his new yardman with a fresh look of dawning interest, and respect. 'How old are you, Mister Nufall?'

'Thirty-three.'

'You've crammed some living into those thirty-three years, I'd say.'

The gardener laughed again, that same soft, deep roll of sound. 'My share, Mister Spencer.'

'Well; it's getting late.' Merritt shoved out his hand again. 'Glad we met,' he said, shook, withdrew his hand, then looked past over where some lights shone from the handsome big fieldstone mansion. 'Good-night.'

As he walked away from the younger man Merritt felt the thoughtful gaze following him. That didn't make him uncomfortable, but the fact that Frederick Nufall had an answer that made sense for everything Merritt had said *did* trouble him, a little.

Of course he was accustomed to Domingo, and although the stableman was wise in his own earthy way, he was not wise the way this new man was, at all.

For once, it seemed, Harold had done something worthwhile for his father. Accidentally, of course, but still worth while.

It never once crossed Merritt's mind that he'd been hell-bent on firing Frederick Nufall, and as he entered the quiet house, he even speculated a little on the fact that Nufall might be a man he could lean on, could rely upon; might in fact be the link between his earlier generation and the current one, which was something his own son had never been for him.

He retired feeling better for the first time since Erin had brought him that message from Harold. If Nufall wouldn't turn out to be another of those fly-by-night employees, now, everything just might possibly turn out fairly well after all.

Chapter Four

THE MAN IN DARK GLASSES

Merritt was waiting on the loggia when Harold's Cadillac turned in down at the road. He turned at a slight sound and found Erin Clancy standing in the opening behind him wearing a freshly starched white dress and with her red hair drawn severely back into a bun.

'I'll have ice in the bar,' she reported, 'and when you're ready I'll have luncheon prepared.'

She didn't await an answer, but turned and walked away, her back very straight. She did not like Harold Spencer, but then Merritt had known that for some time. He didn't make any issue of it with her. In the first place she was more important to his orderly life right now than Harold was. In the second place — well — there were times when Merritt didn't like Harold either.

It was ten o'clock, the sun was high, the day sparkled, and when Harold and the others climbed forth from the car, they took a deep breath of the clean, fragrant air.

Merritt went down to meet them.

Harold introduced his father to the thick-shouldered, black-wavy-haired man wearing the dark glasses, whose lips were a wound in his lower face and whose clothing was both impeccable and very expensive. Esparza smiled thinly as he shook Merritt's hand. He murmured something about Merritt having a beautiful estate, here.

Jacqueline looked more sleek and sophisticated than usual, her hair soft-shiny and tinted a shade of very becoming ash-blonde. She kissed her grandfather's bronzed leathery cheek and squeezed his hand. It was impossible for him not to melt when she did those things; whatever she was now, for ten years they had been wonderful friends. Merritt remembered those years graphically and warmly, whether the sophisticated, beautiful woman in front of him recalled them or not.

Harold was, as usual, calm to the point of boredom. He shook hands with his father, squinted against the reflection of sunlight off the house-front, and said something about the heat as they all started towards the loggia.

Nick Esparza was either just naturally quiet, or preoccupied. He was polite, gave proper answers whenever called upon to speak at all, but otherwise his interest seemed somewhere else.

Even inside the house, he did not remove his dark glasses. His features were thin, but darkly handsome, and it also irked Merritt Spencer that the man was not wearing some garish tie, or some modishly-cut clothes. Esparza could have passed anywhere as a successful, conservative businessman.

Merritt kept up a little running fire of casual conversation while he took them to the barroom, stepped behind the teakwood bar and started mixing drinks. The others seemed perfectly at ease, which annoyed him too because he *didn't* feel that way. In fact, although he understood this meeting to be for the purpose of introducing him to his granddaughter's fiancé, the people across the bar seemed not too concerned about that.

He set up the glasses, looked at his son and said, 'That man Nufall seems very capable, Harold.'

His son smiled down at him as he sipped the highball, an indulgent, disinterested smile. 'Of course he is. I tried to tell you that.'

Jacqueline tasted her drink then put it down. She smiled at her grandfather. 'You told me once that when I got married, you'd decorate the house out here like a Christmas tree.'

Merritt nodded and shot a look at Nick Esparza, who was gazing at Jacqueline without a trace of any emotion in his face.

'Well, Granddad, Nick and I plan to be married next month. On the fifteenth. Do you still want to go to all that work?'

Merritt smiled and nodded again. He had a sick feeling in his chest. 'If you're sure,' he told her, and caught the swift, darting look Esparza turned towards him.

'We're very sure,' Jacqueline said, reaching over to pat one of Merritt's hands that was atop the bar. He looked down; it was the right hand but there was no engagement ring. That, probably, was part of the new morality; engagement rings were stuffy.

Harold, watching his father, moved in as soon as the older man's face seemed to harden slightly. 'I could have the caterers come out and talk to you within the next few days. The thing is — are you up to it? I mean, all the frenzy and —'

Merritt straightened up and flushed. 'Look, if you think sixty is old you'd better remember that age is a mental attitude more than a question of years.'

Harold wasn't taken aback; he had known his father all his life. When the old man got like this Harold just smiled. 'Fine. I'll send them out the first of next month.'

Esparza was gazing at Merritt through his dark glasses. It was impossible to see his eyes through them; the effect, at least in Merritt's view was like looking into the eyes of an over-sized grasshopper.

Jacqueline, sensitive to the suddenly altered atmosphere, said, 'Let's go back to the loggia. It's so peaceful and fragrant out there.'

The men let her lead the way. Nick Esparza, walking beside Merritt, turned and for the first time changed expression. He smiled just the smallest bit, as though Merritt's anger back at the bar amused him. Then he said, 'I'll foot the bill, Mister Spencer.'

Merritt's pique came up again. 'It's her father's responsibility, actually, but since I've been assuming that for him for forty years, I suppose one more time won't kill me, Mister Esparza.'

The fair-skinned but dark-eyed and dark-haired man kept smiling at Merritt. 'It's your ball-game, then,' he said, sounding both disinterested and condescending. 'I'll send along a list of people I'd like to be here. Not very many; maybe a half dozen. I'm not much on ceremony, but then this isn't my play, is it?'

'You might,' said old Merritt drily, 'talk it over with Jackie.'

That tickled Esparza and his grin widened. 'You know, I think we could get along if we tried, Mister Spencer.'

Merritt had no chance to retort. They passed through the wide opening on to the marble loggia, and Jacqueline laughed as she threw her arms wide. It was, Merritt thought, over-acting.

She said, 'I've never seen a place I loved as much as this one.' She whirled. 'Grandad, do you still have the horses?'

He nodded, 'I also still have Domingo. You may remember him; he practically taught you to ride when you were younger.'

'I want to go see them,' she said, not being specific about whether she wanted to see the horses, or the horses *and* Domingo.

Merritt looked at Harold. His son had never liked horses; had in fact never really liked country living. Harold made a grimace and waved a hand. 'Go ahead, by all means,' he said to his daughter. 'But if you don't object I'll stay here in the shade and finish my drink.'

She turned. 'Nick?'

He smiled at her. 'Horses aren't my bag, kid, unless they're running on a track. I'll visit here with your grandfather.' He raised an arm, looked at a golden watch, then continued to smile at Jacqueline as though reminding her of something.

She stood a moment watching the three of them, but finally turned and went hastening along the loggia towards some broad, wide marble steps that led back down to the garden.

The men found chairs and Harold slumped as he always did when he sat. That had irritated his father terribly in years past. Now he hardly heeded it. Both the younger men had brought their highball glasses with them. Esparza drained his, put it aside and said, 'You've spent a fortune here, Mister Spencer. But it must be lonely.'

'Never,' averred Merritt. 'Loneliness is something that comes only when you have bad memories, Mister Esparza.'

Again that indulgent, lean smile appeared as the shiny sun-glasses turned towards Merritt. 'You kind of surprise me, Mister Spencer. I know how you made your money, and the steel industry isn't something that I'd guess also turned out philosophers.'

Merritt snorted, but it was Harold who spoke next. His tone was, as usual, slow and distinct, and a little patronizing. 'You don't know my father, Nick. He has always been a rugged individualist.'

Esparza drew forth a hammered-silver, curved cigarette case, offered it around, got no takers, and lit up. 'Self-mades usually are individualists,' he told Harold, and Merritt wondered if he detected something a little acidy in those words.

There was one thing he had already learned about Nick Esparza; the man's face never revealed anything, not even when he smiled because the smile reflected less amusement than something else, and it would never be possible to know what that was, unless a person knew Esparza himself. And that, Merritt told himself, would be like trying to know a snake; you might *think* you knew something, but you really wouldn't.

'About this marriage,' said Esparza, exhaling bluish smoke. 'She'll want something elaborate, and that suits me. But if we could avoid the show-business personalities it would suit me a lot better.'

Merritt, firmly committed to disliking Nick Esparza, kept getting these little jolts that did not jibe with what he knew this man to be. Personally, he would prefer not to have his place over-run by show-business personalities too.

'Just send me your list,' he told Esparza, his voice less rough. 'I'll get Jacqueline's list from her, and I think I can be trusted to manage.'

Harold frowned. 'Is this her marriage, or just something we sit here arranging between us?'

Esparza smoked, studied the yonder gardens, and said nothing. Merritt, understanding

Esparza's discretion, said, 'If it were left to you, Harold, I'd have to lay in a stock of whisky as well as food.'

Harold groaned and rolled his eyes. Then he turned and looked hard at Esparza. 'How about the Las Vegas and Reno crowd?'

'Only a few,' replied the dark man. 'Like I said before, Mister Spencer, only a half dozen or so. I'll get you a copy of the list.' Then Esparza leaned to kill his smoke in an ashtray and said, 'She's got some bums for friends from the theatre. They aren't her friends but she doesn't know it yet; won't find it out until they try to cut her throat. Maybe it's a little soon to start doing it, but I'm going to eliminate those people sooner or later. Sooner might be best.' He leaned back and looked at Harold. 'Okay?'

Harold did not respond and Merritt's doubts about Esparza turned to plain bafflement. There were some things about this man he agreed with; the toughness, for one thing, the limited conversation for another. But what bothered him most now was the *degree* of toughness. Was Esparza going to dominate Jacqueline's life or guide it?

Again, he would have to know the man a lot better than he did now, to arrive at the answers he needed. He asked if either of them would care for another drink. Harold agreed, and arose to take their glasses back to the bar and refill them himself. That left Esparza alone with Merritt.

The younger man sighed and gave his head a slight shake. 'Life starts getting complicated as soon as you let it lean on you a little, Mister Spencer. Frankly, I'm not the marrying kind.'

Merritt was startled. He would have agreed that Esparza was not the kind of man to show much emotion, but all that might have meant was that he kept himself under a tight rein. But this remark was a statement that left little doubt.

'Then why are you marrying my granddaughter?' he asked.

'A man gets to a certain age, Mister Spencer, and he's got it made — so it's time. Everyone should have a son.'

Merritt thought that over. Leaving out of consideration his own mixed feelings on this score, Esparza's reason for marrying seemed as cold, as scheming, as the man's general attitude implied he would be about most things, and whether a man was tough-minded like Merritt or not, there happened to be something infinitely more important as a reason for wanting to marry than just the practical aspect of a son.

Esparza turned, evidently attracted by Merritt's long silence. They looked at one another for a moment then Esparza said, 'You don't have to figure me out, Mister Spencer. If Jacqueline is satisfied, that's all that should matter to you.'

Now, finally, Merritt was beginning to flesh-out his impression of this quiet, confident, ruthless man, and it didn't gratify him very much to realize that what he had made up his mind about, before ever meeting Nick Esparza, was right.

Chapter Five

THE GARDENER AND THE LADY

There was an old belief, in some areas, that a goat should always be kept with the horses, then, if colic or distemper came along, it would settle upon the goat and spare the horses.

Goats, like sheep, being highly susceptible to bronchial upsets, very often had colds, so it wasn't difficult to understand how that superstition came into being; the goat out in the pasture with the horses had the sniffles and a runny nose, while the horses were quite healthy.

Domingo Salazar had for several years had a goat around the stables and Merritt Spencer was content to let him keep the beast. But the day Erin Clancy was hanging blankets out to sun them and the goat, mistaking her for an intruder perhaps, caught her from behind with a great bunt, marked the beginning of the end of the goat's tenure at the estate.

The pen and goat-house — built like a dog-kennel only larger — were still there, but now a stray cat had taken up residence there. She had sore eyes, a mangy coat, and had been badly mauled recently, when Domingo first discovered her in the goat-house. Many scratches and much meat and milk later, he had cured her ailments, restored her spirit, and now she lay in the tall grass, eyes closed to slits, great belly distended, watching Jacqueline approach.

Domingo was out in the pasture cleaning water troughs and thus missed her entirely. Fred Nufall saw her long before she reached the stables over near his quarters where he was staking up a droopy little tree someone else had planted — probably Domingo, the reluctant gardener — and had then neglected.

He stood in shadows watching her stride, which was long, and her supple grace, which was worth watching. Finally, when she saw him and headed up towards him, Fred turned back to finish staking the little tree. He could guess who she was without any difficulty, and had ample time to adjust to a meeting, which was inevitable, before she stopped nearby, smiled and explained that she was Merritt's granddaughter, and wished to see Domingo and the horses.

Domingo, he told her, was out in the pasture, and only two of the horses were stalled, the others were turned out. He was pleasant towards her without smiling. He even offered to go find Domingo for her. She declined that offer with thanks, then, after studying Fred a bit, asked how long he'd been with her grandfather.

That time he smiled. 'Two days.'

'Are you a horseman?'

He finished securing the little tree to its stake. 'A lot of things,' he said, 'but not that.

I'm the yardman.'

She seemed to be interested. As she later had occasion to remark, his English was good, his attitude just a shade superior, his looks definitely different from those of the usual yardman.

'Do you like it here?' she asked, and he turned to gaze at her.

'I like it fine — after just two days.' He no longer smiled. His gaze wasn't hostile but neither was it brimming with amiability. 'Anything else?'

She blushed, shook her head, turned and walked through the breezeway to the courtyard of the stables, beyond his sight.

It was near enough to the end of his work-day for him to gather up tools and head for the shed to leave them. It was on his way back, passing across the open end of the tanbarked stable courtyard that he saw her again. She was sitting slumped and dejected upon a wooden bench outside one of the occupied stalls, looking small and unhappy. He didn't even hesitate, but turned and walked down towards her. It was quiet in the stable area. There were soft shadows lying within the courtyard and a drowsing horse had its head hung over the top of a stall door, as still as stone.

He stopped and said, 'Odd thing about life, Miss Spencer; the things we grew up with never quite leave us.'

She raised her face. It was an odd thing for a perfect stranger to say. 'Meaning?'

'If a kid grows up loving the outdoors, horses, green fields, blue skies and fresh air, maybe those things don't seem important later on; maybe the kid goes to the city and gets caught up in the rat-race of proving something. Then, sometime, the urge to go back comes over this kid, fully grown now, and all kinds of inner conflicts ensue.'

She gazed steadily at him, then said, 'You ought to write a book.'

He grinned. 'I've thought of it. But who would buy a couple hundred pages of telling people what they already know?'

'No one,' she said tartly.

'Okay,' he said quietly. 'Now we've both insulted each other. So let's get back to the subject.'

'No thanks,' she retorted, and stood up, glanced at her wrist then said, 'My grandfather always did hire the oddest people out here.'

'They can't be any more odd than the ones who visit him out here.'

Her blue-grey eyes began to smoulder. 'Don't you have something to do; some more trees to brace-up, or something?'

'Not a thing more until tomorrow morning.' He stepped over against an upright-post and leaned there. 'It's always more fun to mind someone else's business than one's own business.'

She didn't permit him to add more to that. 'For you, perhaps, but for me — no.'

He appraised her with candid admiration.

'What I see in you is a little girl, probably with pigtails, riding hell-for-leather among the trees. Then there is an interlude when you start believing all the things people who love you have told you — and that's the beginning of the change.'

She had pink in her face again, and the anger that had been kindling in her eyes was brighter too. 'And you, Mister Whatever-your-name-is — a man of the world who has always wanted to be just a gardener on some large estate.'

He ignored the sarcasm and nodded. 'That's pretty close. But I've got it and you haven't.'

'Haven't got what?'

'This,' he replied, with a gesture, 'the peace and quiet and fresh air. So instead of trying to find the compromise you've got to rush from one frustration to another.'

That did it. She stiffened and lashed back at him with words that were designed to sting. 'That might be better than running away and hiding, than being afraid of life and coming hat-in-hand to an old man who would hire you as a menial so your bruises could be nursed behind someone else's skirts — or pants!'

He remained relaxed against the upright-post, silent until she'd spent the first rush of her anger. 'It might be better,' he agreed quietly. 'At least it would give a person time to gather his thoughts together. The other way, rushing into other messes, would only compound the difficulties.'

She was losing to him. Obviously, she couldn't

anger him, and just as obviously he had thought all this out before, so his answers were sensible and calm while hers were neither.

'Suppose my grandfather fired you. Then where would you crawl away to pity yourself?'

'There is always a place, Miss Spencer, if a man needs to find one. As for him firing me — he might. But I just don't see you as the kind of person you're trying to make me think you are.'

'Don't make that mistake, Mister Whatever-your-name-is.'

'Nufall. Fred Nufall. And I'm not making a mistake. *You* are making them, though.'

'I see. You are minding my business instead of your own.'

'Miss Spencer, it's a much smaller world out here. That tree I was bracing up when you came along, is important. There's an alleycat about to have kittens that is important. When it rains and when it doesn't rain are important. The people are important — including you — so other people take an interest. It's not like it is in the city where no one knows or cares, or else they see you as some kind of threat. I know a few things about you. Not bad things. Kind of stupid, but not bad. And out here I'm your friend while in the city whether you lived or died, married or remained single, wouldn't mean a thing to me.'

Jacqueline's anger subsided but not the indignation, it remained as strong as before, and it tinted her words, but without the anger they were more quiet. 'Whatever you know about me,

Mister Nufall, you got second or third hand, which means it can't be very accurate. As for the stupid things — you don't know what you're talking about.'

'You were sitting here looking unhappy, Miss Spencer. Well, I've seen my share of women about to be married, and most of them were walking on clouds.'

'I see. So that's a stupid thing — my getting married.'

'You said it, lady, not I.'

'You are impossible, Mister Nufall. You are a busybody, a fool, and . . . oh, never mind!' She stepped past him and walked swiftly out of the stable courtyard.

He turned and watched her depart. When she was lost to sight around the corner of the stable, he straightened up and ambled after her as far as the sunshiny area beyond the courtyard. There, he watched her until she was lost again in shadows over through the trees towards the main house.

Domingo Salazar came walking in carrying some tools; he leaned against the side of the stable while he removed his old hat and pushed sweat off his dark forehead with a soiled sleeve.

'Wasn't that Mister Spencer's granddaughter?' he asked, attracting Nufall's attention away from the distant, fading silhouette.

Nufall nodded. 'It was. And we had an argument.'

Domingo's black eyes jumped to Nufall's face,

but until he'd replaced the old hat he was silent. Then he said, 'Why? She is the apple of the old man's eye. He won't like it that you argued with her. Anyway, what could you two argue about, you don't even know her?'

Nufall smiled at Salazar. 'That's true. I guess I was just being what she called me — a busybody.'

Domingo blinked. 'She called you that? I've known her ever since she was a little kid with a smile bigger than her face. I think if she said that to you, there must have been a reason.'

'There was, Domingo. She had a good reason. I stuck my big nose in where it had no business, but you see, back a few years I got in the habit of prowling barracks and picking out the homesick lads and taking them out for a beer and a heart-to-heart. It didn't always help them, but sometimes it did. The objective was to keep them from doing something stupid — like going over the hill, which would land them in *real* trouble. Well; there she sat, about to be married, looking as unhappy as some apron-string recruit, so I just naturally went over to talk to her.'

Domingo, who had never been a soldier, understood the gist of all this, but it still made him feel uncomfortable. 'Mister Spencer will come calling on you after supper,' he predicted with a sad-eyed look of certainty and resignation. 'Damn; just when I was sure everything would work out and I wouldn't have to plant any more flowers.'

Nufall laughed, slapped Salazar on the back

and said, 'How would you like a tall glass of chilled beer? Come along; I've got some in my quarters.'

Domingo did not protest because he had been thinking of cold beer for over an hour, out there in the pasture where the heat lay in layers, but this other thing bothered him almost enough to make even the anticipation of the beer diminish in importance.

'Maybe if you apologized to the old man,' he said, as they stopped outside Nufall's quarters. 'And I could hint that maybe I'd quit if I had to go back to gardening again.'

Nufall said nothing more until he'd got their glasses of beer, had returned to the shady place out front where there were a couple of steel chairs for them to sit on and relax in the early twilight. But then he said, 'Don't you get involved. Anyway, if I read the girl right, she won't even tell her grandfather.'

Domingo drank thirstily, seemed to get fresh energy from the amber liquid, and removed his hat, let it drop to the black pavement underfoot, then shook his head.

'She used to run to him with everything, when she was a child.'

'Domingo,' mused Nufall, gazing off in the direction the beautiful girl had gone, 'if there is one thing Miss Spencer is *not,* it's a child.'

Chapter Six

A TALK BY STARLIGHT

Domingo's prediction was correct. Merritt Spencer came strolling down through the warm night to the stable-area after dinner and long after his visitors had departed.

But Domingo didn't know it; he was in his room watching television, neither looked up as Merritt passed his open front door, nor heard the sound of his employer's footfalls.

Fred, though, was sitting outside his quarters and had seen Merritt coming long before he even got close. Fred had showered, had given up on the television, and was out there sitting sprawled and easy, smoking a long-stemmed pipe with a sterling band, when Merritt came up, halted, and leaned upon the cross-piece between a pair of overhang uprights as he squinted through dark shadows and said, 'Good evening, Fred.'

It was the first time he'd used Nufall's first name. Fred removed the pipe and nodded, then he reached to push a chair around for his employer, but Merritt remained comfortably leaning upon the cross-piece.

'You made quite an impression on my granddaughter this afternoon,' exclaimed Merritt.

Fred smiled softly in the gloom. 'It worked both ways, Mister Spencer.'

'I would imagine. But I couldn't quite make up my mind whether she had been insulted, or just argued with.'

'She didn't tell you?'

'No.'

'Well, Mister Spencer, I guess it was some of both. And I told her I didn't think she'd really ask you to fire me, or even tell you I'd insulted her.'

'You sized her up pretty well, eh?'

'Better than she sized me up, Mister Spencer, but then I've been at the sizing-up business a lot longer.' Fred put the pipe behind him upon a windowsill, squared up slightly in the chair and gazed serenely at the older man. 'She is a very beautiful woman, Mister Spencer. I don't blame Esparza or any man for wanting to marry her. But it won't last.'

'The beauty?'

'The marriage.'

Merritt shifted stance a little, fished through his pockets until he found his pipe, then he said, 'What kind of tobacco do you smoke?'

Fred handed over his pouch without answering. As Merritt began tamping the pipe-bowl Fred said, 'If this is a little awkward for you, I can quit and make it easier.'

Merritt finished stuffing his pipe-bowl, lit a match and got up a fine head of smoke before attempting to speak again. 'Fred, I was in business forty years, man and boy; firing people stopped bothering me after the first ten years. And don't think you ever have to make things easy for me.'

Nufall's perfect teeth shone white in the gloom. 'Then you'll want to know exactly what happened down here this afternoon.'

'Yes.'

Fred told him, almost word for word, and the only way anyone could have known Merritt was even listening was by those little fat puffs of smoke that arose from time to time. Then, when the recital was over, Merritt stepped around the chair Nufall had offered earlier, sat down and crossed his legs to be thoroughly comfortable. Finally he spoke.

'Too bad Esparza didn't walk down here with her. I'd like to have had you size him up too. You hit the nail on the head with Jacqueline — I think — although we've grown pretty far apart the past few years. But this Esparza — I can't quite make him out. One thing I know — he's as hard as iron. The other thing I *suspect* is that he's also as cold as a dead fish.'

'As a husband . . . ?'

'That, my boy, is the hell of it. I just don't know.'

'Well, I'll tell you, Mister Spencer. Your granddaughter isn't in love with him, so if he marries her, and if he's fairly perceptive, he's going to learn that darned quick. Then, if he's a conceited man, he's going to have one badly bruised ego, which means he isn't going to look upon this wife of his as anything worth respecting.'

'You're sure she doesn't love him?'

'I'm sure, sir.'

'Then tell me something, Fred, why in the hell did she ask me to get the house ready for their wedding the fifteenth of next month?'

Fred was slow at answering that. He considered his feet for a moment, then asked a question. 'Just how badly do you really want an answer to that?'

Merritt puffed, pulled the pipe from his lips and blew smoke. 'What have you in mind?'

'A couple of days off.'

'You've got 'em. Anything else?'

'The use of your car.'

'You've got that too. Need some cash?'

'No.'

The older man plugged the pipe back into his mouth and resumed his puffing as though they'd been discussing something a lot less serious than what they had been talking about, loosened slightly in the chair and finally sighed.

'You'll know how to go about this, I take it?'

'I know, Mister Spencer.'

Merritt got quiet again for another long interval. 'She'll disown me if you make it too obvious, Fred.'

'Mister Spencer I said I knew how to go about it.'

For the last time Merritt retreated into his long silence. During this interval his pipe went out so he knocked it empty against the uprightpost then dropped it into a pocket, hitched forward on the chair and said, 'Care to come up to the house with me and have a nightcap?'

Fred and the older man exchanged a tough look, then Nufall gently shook his head. 'No disrespect intended, Mister Spencer.'

Merritt slapped his lean legs, arose and said, 'Sure not. Well; I'll have to coddle Domingo while you're gone.' He smiled. 'I may have the hardest job of the two of us, at that. Good-night.'

Nufall arose and watched his employer go ambling back through the patches of starlight and shadow. He got the pipe he'd abandoned, cleaned it carefully into a flowerbed, then took a little stroll out back of the stables and down to one of the white-painted paddock fences where he could see some horses sleeping standing up beneath a giant oak tree.

'Hey!'

He turned. Domingo was padding silently across the warm grass. 'You had a visitor just like I figured. And now I'm back to watering the flowers again, eh?'

Nufall laughed at Salazar's expression. 'No, he didn't fire me. But I'll be gone a couple of days, so you may have to water the flowers anyway.'

Domingo leaned on the fence sideways so he could see the taller man's face. 'Gone? He sent you to do an errand?'

'I guess you could call it that, Domingo. There's something fishy about this marriage between his granddaughter and Esparza. I'm going up to the city and see what I can nose out.'

'You know something, Fred? You're getting in a little deeper every time you open your mouth.'

'Yeah. Well; that's always been one of my major problems.' Nufall gazed at Salazar. 'You like Merritt Spencer?'

'Sure. He's tough, but the pay is good, he never stares over your shoulder, and — well — if I didn't like him I wouldn't still be here after all these years. That answer you?'

Fred nodded. 'I kind of like him too, Domingo.'

'After only two days?'

'Haven't you ever known people who weren't so complicated you couldn't figure them out in only two days?'

'Yes, I suppose so. But I still think you're getting in too deep. Look; if a man is a gardener, and if he's content to be that, maybe it's not so smart being anything else.'

'I just told you — that's one of my problems. Like the lovely lady said, I'm a busybody.' Fred grinned. 'How about another cold beer?'

'Sure. How much of that stuff did you bring here with you?'

They smiled at each other, turned and started back towards the stable. Domingo Salazar had just got to know one of those people it was possible to get to know, and to like, in only a couple of days. But he still felt that Fred Nufall was riding for a fall. Personally, although he'd been friendly with his employer for a long time, he still would have shied away from any kind of close relationship. A man who worked for another man was supposed to know his place, and to stay in it. Otherwise he had to go hunt a new job sooner or later.

But there was one thing that caused him a little doubt, encouraged him to some personal and private speculation: Fred Nufall was no more a common labourer than he, Domingo Salazar, was a rich estate owner. There might be something in that which would save Fred from losing his job, and Domingo didn't want him to get fired. Not only was his chilled beer very good, but he was an easy, relaxed person to be around.

While they were standing outside in the pleasant warmth and pewter light, Domingo said, 'I'll tell you something, Fred: Now this is simply the opinion of an ignorant horseman who has no education and has never been married or had children.'

'Shoot.'

'When she was young girl hanging around my stable whatever I told her she believed, and whenever I showed her the right way to do something, like holding her reins or getting her animal started off in the right lead, she listened.'

'So? What are you saying, that she's smart?'

'No. What I'm saying is that she has never really had a father.'

Nufall finished his beer, crushed the can in one hand, and blew out a great breath. 'Thanks,

Domingo. I'll remember that.'

'It is nothing, really. Anyway, now she's an actress on the stage, a grown woman, and doesn't even remember old Domingo.'

'You're wrong. The first thing she asked when she was here this afternoon was where you were?'

Domingo looked up. 'Did she?'

Fred smiled at the older, shorter man. 'Too bad you never had kids, Domingo. Now go on back and watch your television. Good-night.'

Later, in the unlighted darkness of his own quarters, Fred got ready for bed. It was almost ten o'clock, which was late for men to stay up who worked at physical labour.

But he wasn't sleepy.

Two days at the Spencer estate and he was involved up to the neck. Well; no matter where he was, it usually happened that way.

He didn't mind at all, and although he understood Domingo's fears and appreciated his misgivings, he also knew something that perhaps, even after all those years, Domingo *didn't* know about his employer: Merritt Spencer might have a few years on him, but he was still just as practical, tough and resourceful as a man half his age. A man's man, he was. People had often said the same thing about Fred Nufall — usually punctuating it with profanity.

As for doing what he'd proposed, he anticipated no difficulty there. No one at the Spencer estate knew it, but Fred Nufall had done similar things, only in much more hazardous spots of the world, and along far more dangerous lines.

He went to bed, finally, and lay in the silent darkness remembering how Jacqueline Spencer's gunmetal eyes had flashed fire at him, and he sighed, because there had been women in his life, but this one, for some reason he didn't bother trying to analyse, was very different.

Why that should be, was impossible to pin down. He'd known women nearly as beautiful, certainly as liable to inherit wealth, and equally as sleekly sophisticated. Maybe it was because Jacqueline Spencer, although very sophisticated, didn't radiate the cynical hardness of most beautiful women. Maybe it was because that little pigtailed girl he'd glimpsed, briefly there in the stable courtyard, had been lacking in those other sleek women.

He gave up his thoughts with a grunt, turned on to his side and went to sleep.

Chapter Seven

TO THE CITY AND BACK

At one time the city of Chicago ended not very far across the river beyond the Wrigley building, but that had been before Fred Nufall ever saw it. Now, it ran out as far as the former suburb of Evanston without any intervals of open ground. It also went beyond Evanston, poured out and around the exclusive and wealthy utopia of Kenilworth — not quite so utopian any more — then gobbled up Glencoe — once called Glencohen — and after that it just kind of ran out like water over sand until it petered out in the countryside.

It was for the most part a dirty, gritty city where the wind blew in off Lake Michigan in wintertime with a chill that went all the way to the marrow, and where in summertime it reeled under a brassy kind of flawless heat that, once it arrived, didn't depart until late autumn.

It was noisy as well as huge and dirty, but each neighbourhood was rather like a village; people knew what was going on, who was doing what, and where, within their own perimeter. Beyond those areas, people were in an alien place.

State Street had miles of theatres, office buildings, and just beyond it stood the white towers of a traditionally clean banker's and broker's building over on Washington Street.

People in certain parts of State Street who made their living from the theatres, could name every prominent actor or actress going back twenty years. They could also give the background gossip about which shows were financed by which rich angels — showgirls' lovers — and which shows had mob money in them, as well as the ones, honest though they might be, and dedicated to true art, were going to go belly-up.

To get this information was easy; all one had to do was spend money in one of the garish little go-down nightclubs, or strike up an acquaintance with some thirsty down-and-outer, the way Fred did his first evening in the city.

The bum's name was Lockhart. Charles Lockhart, and so he said with a perfectly solemn face, there hadn't been a baritone in the country who could hold a candle to him in the thirties, then that lousy war had to come along to ruin everything. By the time Charles Lockhart got back from trying to drink France and Germany dry, his voice, like his contacts, were gone. So now he worked the stage doors keeping out the crashers, and as he said, it was a living. Not a very good one because it was no longer possible to catch a few dollars on the side lining up dates.

'In the old days,' he explained over his fifth very dry martini, 'you could take their ten-spot to set up a date, then just slip out the front way and leave 'em to cuss. But they aren't sports about those things any more. You try that today, and the next night they are back, maybe with a buddy, and they mug you.'

It wasn't, Fred agreed, like it used to be, and pressed a ten-dollar note into Lockhart's palm while he sat in the smoke-hazed little booth still working on his first beer.

'Tell me about this babe, Francesca,' he said, and watched Lockhart down the fifth martini without a quiver.

'Who?'

'Francesca. The dancer next door on the Tivoli Theatre.'

'Oh her. Yeah. Say, she's really put together isn't she? Well, have you caught the act?'

Fred nodded.

'Pretty gruesome isn't it?'

Fred gave another nod and when the waiter came to refill Lockhart's glass, Fred held on to his beer mug to prevent it being swept up too. After the waiter had departed Lockhart leaned and leered.

'I never could understand why they still believe they can act or sing or dance when they haven't got anything at all. Good Lord, you ought to know, hadn't you?'

'It would seem that way,' replied Fred, trying to gauge the degree of drunkenness in the man across from him, and deciding that the sixth martini ought to just about stiffen Lockhart, so if any good answers were to be elicited it might be best to press right along. 'But if she can't dance or act, then what's keeping her up there on the stage?'

Lockhart grinned widely. 'Brother, you can't be that dumb. Nick Esparza's keeping her up there. He owns a piece of the show. I don't know why; from what I've picked up around town Esparza backs some good rackets, and this show is a real stinker. It loses money hand over fist. So — it's got to be Francesca, don't it? I mean, she's got to be the answer.'

'He's going to marry her.'

Lockhart nodded. 'How about that? I heard it a week or so ago. Now why in hell would a guy with everything going for him want to marry this girl, will you tell me that?'

'Can't,' said Fred, paying the waiter for Lockhart's sixth very dry martini. 'You ought to know why he'd marry her.'

'But I don't. The usual reasons don't apply. I mean, a guy like Nick Esparza can have his pick, he don't have to marry them. You see? But maybe it's some kind of front for him.' Lockhart lifted the glass but had to put it down quickly because his hand was beginning to shake. Then he said, 'But I can tell you one thing: He's bought a new show and is going all the way up to Broadway in New York City with it, starring this Francesca. It's crazy, I know. Absolutely crazy. Man, that girl won't be able to stay alive in New York for one lousy week, even with Esparza's money riding on her. But what's even crazier is that he'd do something this dumb. He knows the babe can't act.' Lockhart threw up his arms as though this entire affair were just too horrifying for additional exploration, then he lunged for the glass, got up, tipped at the right angle, and dropped the sixth very dry martini right, straight, down.

That time the shudder hit him, and Fred reached to pat his shoulder, then got up and moved off into the crowd. Lockhart would be a piece of human driftwood for the balance of the night.

There were two things left to learn but Fred didn't feel like making the effort. He knew that whatever the answers were, he wasn't going to like them.

Why was Esparza doing this, and what interested Fred much more, but in a morbid way, why was Jacqueline Spencer going along with him; even up to the point of marrying him?

A taxi took him away from the Loop and over to one of the better hotels where he checked in for the night. The following morning he went back to the neighbourhood of the Tivoli Theatre, where Jacqueline, as Francesca, did her bit of 'interpretive art', as it was called on the marquee.

There, he struck up a conversation with a grey and grizzled man with sad eyes and a disillusioned face, who operated a news-stand, and here, finally, he picked up a little worthwhile information.

Francesca, said this knowledgeable and cynical individual, was going to marry Nick Esparza because he'd promised her the lead in his New York show.

Fred left a ten dollar note lying atop a stack of newspapers and when the grizzled man looked from that up to his face, Fred said, 'You're doing fine. Now tell me why *he* is marrying *her?*'

'That is even easier, mister. She's got class. You know; her father's a millionaire businessman, highly respected, belongs to the best clubs, stuff like that. And her grandfather is old Merritt Spencer who used to just have to frown around this city, and everyone crawled into a hole. Them folks isn't just rich, they got class, you see; real, upper class, class.'

Fred thought that over. Maybe it was correct and then again maybe it wasn't. He couldn't really be definitive because he did not know Nick Esparza that well.

When he left the news-stand he had a magazine about show-business personalities the newsy had sold him — over and above the ten-spot of course — in which there was a brief article about the forthcoming nuptials between socialite-showgirl Jacqueline (Francesca) Spencer, and Nick Esparza, complete with a publicity photograph of Jacqueline in a very scanty costume.

He could have hung around Chicago the balance of that day, but he thought he had about all Merritt Spencer wanted, so he went back to the car and drove carefully out through the screeching tumult of Chicago until he found an expressway, then sped away as fast as he could, with safety.

The shadows were down on all sides before he got anywhere near the estate, and before he reached the electric wrought-iron front gates, it was full night.

He put the car up, saw only one light in the main house, and that in back where Erin Clancy had quarters, so he went down to his own quarters at the stable.

There, he found Domingo down on his hands and knees with a flashlight by the goat-house, so engrossed that until Fred spoke Domingo didn't know he was there.

'What's the trouble?'

Domingo gave a little start, then raised the flashlight. 'The cat is having her kittens.'

'Well; they've been doing that for five thousand years, haven't they?'

'Not this way. Go change into your work clothes and come back to hold the light for me. The cat is having trouble.'

'Do you know what to do, Domingo?'

'Yes, of course. Go change your clothes.'

Fred went obediently along to his quarters, changed, left his valise, the magazine, even the personality that went with his city-clothes, then hastened back.

Domingo was leaning back on his haunches wiping perspiration from his face with a soiled handkerchief. 'It's all over,' he said.

Fred took the flashlight and looked down. There were tiny, wet, snuffling little animals and rolling all around the mother cat. She was wet too, and although she looked ominously gaunt and exhausted, she nevertheless was licking her progeny.

'Seven,' Fred said, and grinned. 'It looks like it was harder on you than it was on their mother.'

Domingo said something under his breath in Spanish, then let go a big, rattling sigh. 'Did you happen to bring back any more of that beer you drink from the city?'

'Sure. In my valise. But it's not cold.'

'It's wet,' groaned Salazar, struggling to his feet. 'This time I'll pay you. I don't want to always be drinking your beer for nothing.'

They stood for a moment longer watching the cat work over her kittens, then they retreated, made certain the steel gate to the little enclosure was locked so that no stray night-prowling dog or other cat could get in, then went down the stable-walk to Fred's quarters where the beer was dug out, poured, and handed over.

Domingo saw the magazine, flicked it open to the correct page, sipped tepid beer and studied the picture of Jacqueline, and finally read the article. It took quite a while for him to recover from his recent ordeal as midwife, but eventually he tossed down the magazine, followed Fred back outside where it was cooler, and as he sank into a chair he said, 'Well; you weren't gone two full days, so you got what you were after, no?'

Fred lit his pipe. 'I got *something,* yes, but this seems to be one of those riddles that when you get the first answer, it only poses another question.'

Domingo finished his beer and finally smiled. 'What a day! Well, is it a secret?'

'Not especially, Domingo, as long as you keep it to yourself. Esparza's going to marry her because of who she is — daughter and granddaughter of the Spencer millions. She is going to marry him because he's agreed to star her in a Broadway production.'

'She can't act, Fred, she can't even dance very well.'

'Then each one is using the other one, aren't they? And one morning they will both wake up feeling a little sick.'

Domingo slumped in his chair, ran a hand through his curly black hair and said, 'Hell. It's all wrong for her. It will ruin her life.'

'Only a year or two of it,' mused Fred. 'Maybe she's got that coming.'

'What are you talking about? Listen to me; it's not *her* fault. What kind of a father did she have, what kind of a home-life, always in those expensive boarding schools!'

Fred looked at Salazar without speaking for a long time, then he said, 'Domingo; she's over twenty. Maybe you can blame *some* things on environment, but if she persists in being the spoiled, headstrong, foolish rich girl — then it's her bed of thorns.' He stood up. 'See you in the morning . . . And congratulations on becoming a father of seven.'

Chapter Eight

A CONSPIRACY

Merritt was waiting when Fred got back from breakfast. He had seen that the car was in its garage.

They went inside Fred's little sitting-room and Fred told him what he had picked up in the city. Merritt sat gazing at the photograph in the magazine. He listened carefully to all Fred had to report, then he also read that brief article in the magazine.

When Fred was finished, Merritt tossed the magazine away with a growl. 'It's hard to believe,' he said, 'that Jacqueline, who always seemed to me to be such a bright and sensible girl, would marry this man just to be able to play a part in a stage production.'

'Mister Spencer, I don't think that's so unusual. The idea behind it seems to be that if an actress is willing to pay any price and can get someone with money to back her in a Broadway production, then she is on her way to fame and stardom. And of course, once she's well launched, she can then shed the man who got her started.'

Merritt couldn't hide how he felt about that.

'She couldn't be that depraved, Fred.'

Nufall, standing by the rear-wall window, could see Domingo out there in one of the pastures. He idly watched Salazar, not commenting on Merritt's last remark.

Merritt stood up, scowled and said, 'All right. What do you suggest?'

Fred turned. 'Suggest?'

'Well; you went up there and found things out. You know as much — even more — about all this than I do. So what do you suggest we do.'

'Look, Mister Spencer, I'm the yardman here. This other thing is your ball of wax. I went up there because you wanted a little information. That's all.'

Merritt stood gazing at the larger and younger man with no indication of disapproval. For a while he simply stood, but eventually he said, 'Fred, I've got to get her out here and find out if she really is doing something as contemptible as that. But of course she won't tell *me.*'

'Probably not. Not very many people cheerfully admit to being rats, Mister Spencer.'

'But she will tell *you!*'

Fred went to a table, got his pipe and pouch and went to work. The old man had led him into that trap as neat as he pleased. And he was probably correct, too. With her grandfather, Jacqueline would have a bond of affection, but with Fred Nufall, whom she already disliked, she would get angry with only a little prodding.

The older man waited until he'd lit up and was

smoking before saying, 'I'll double your wages.'

Fred returned to the window and saw that Domingo was no longer out in the pasture. He could guess where he'd be now: with the cats at the goat-house. He turned back and nodded.

'All right. You know damned well where this is going to lead. If I stepped out right now it'd be your affair, but if I do what you want this time, I'll be in it up to my neck from here on, and no matter what happens.'

Merritt smiled, relieved. As he went to the door he said, 'I'll get her out here today or tomorrow. I'll let you know which it'll be,' then he left the room and Fred heard him walking swiftly away.

Later, when he met Domingo at the goat-house putting a dish of milk inside for the cat, Salazar looked up a trifle sceptically and said, 'I told you — you're leading with your chin. Mister Spencer passed me a few minutes ago looking happy about something. It couldn't be about the information you brought back, so it had to be something else the two of you have cooked up. I told you, Fred, you're only going to get in so deep you won't be able to get out again.'

Fred sank to one knee beside Domingo and watched the mother-cat drink the milk with a great thirst. 'Domingo, it's hard not to be a fatalist sometimes. A man seems to be born under some kind of sign. No matter where he goes or what he does, there is a kind of pattern that always seems to work out for him. If he lived with trouble, believe me he can't escape it. Maybe he becomes a gardener, but even then, when he has no troubles of his own, trouble comes from other directions. You understand?'

'I understand,' sighed Domingo. 'Well; I wish you well, and if I can help . . .'

They parted for the balance of the day, Domingo going back to his work around the stable, Fred heading for the rose garden on the north side of the mansion where rose-scent and tree-shade made a peaceful, quiet and pleasant place to work.

That evening, after Fred had showered and changed Merritt came down to inform him he'd got hold of Harold and had made him promise to drive out the next morning — and bring Jacqueline.

'It wasn't very simple; Harold doesn't like the country, and it's a long drive. But anyway, I'll try and engineer it so he stays up at the house with me, while Jacqueline comes down here. Maybe I can talk her into going for a horseback ride. By the way, do you ride?'

'After a fashion,' said Fred. 'But not in her league.'

'If she rides off you might take a horse and —'

'Mister Spencer, you just send her down here. I'll do the rest.'

That was how matters stood that evening, and after dinner when Fred and Domingo were sitting out in the gloaming, Fred mentioned the possibility of Merritt Spencer's granddaughter arriving the following morning, and that she might want to go for a ride, and he might want to ride with her.

Domingo nodded, his attitude still one of melancholy over the entire affair, but he said, 'I'll saddle an extra and leave him cross-tied in a stall. By the way, can you ride?'

Fred gave the same reply to Domingo he'd given their employer, and Domingo shrugged, 'It won't matter; I'll saddle for you the gentlest horse we have.'

They spent an agreeable hour visiting after that was settled, then both went off to their quarters.

It was a hot night. Pleasant enough out-of-doors but close and hot inside. Fred slept as though heat didn't really bother him very much, which it didn't, and at the first blush of dawn he was up and stirring.

He met Domingo right after Erin had rung the breakfast bell, and they went together to see how the cats were getting along. The kittens, still with their eyes sealed, were crawling over each other and their mother, tiny tails erect, sleek little tiger-striped bodies as round and furry as could be.

The mother-cat was proud of her offspring. She was also hungry, so Domingo said he'd bring back something from the house, then they went on.

It was going to be a hot day. Domingo, after making a critical examination of the sky, said he thought that by afternoon there would be rainclouds. It was not unusual for summer thundershowers to arrive in the hot afternoons. They cooled the world off for a short while, but after the sun had returned there was a steamy kind of humidity to the atmosphere that made it difficult for people to exert much energy.

But thus far in the new day the heat was less, the air was fresh and clean, and as they got closer to Erin Clancy's big kitchen, the fragrance of summertime was overwhelmed with the equally pleasant fragrance of breakfast bacon and coffee.

Fred did not see Mister Spencer again that day, after catching a glimpse of him at the house, but he did not particularly wish to see him in any case, for although Mister Spencer meant well, he tended to be overly solicitous and that could be annoying.

As for Fred's strategy, he had none. It was not, in his opinion, that critical a rendezvous. No one's life was at stake, no great issues were involved. The girl would arrive, and if her grandfather failed to get her down to the stables, why then that would be the end of it. If he *did* manage to get her down there, Fred would take it from there, managing to spark her dislike of him without much effort.

He smiled to himself as he worked with a drooping hydrangea bush that was supposed to grow up one side of the stable, and which suffered from an excess of water, the careless residue of Domingo's vigorous horse-blanket-washing interludes.

As he ditched for proper drainage, leading the water away from the bush, he recalled how Spencer's granddaughter had last looked at him; as though if she'd had a horsewhip she'd have struck him.

There was fire in her, and definite spirit. It was hard to believe she'd sell her soul so easily, having that kind of character. On the other hand, he had no idea just how much she wanted to succeed as an actress.

That, of course, would be the difference.

He also speculated on the aftermath even if they managed to scotch her romance with Nick Esparza. If she really wished to be an actress above everything else, wouldn't she still struggle towards that goal?

He tried to imagine some way to convince her that she lacked the talent. But what he already knew about women inclined him to believe that no one, least of all some man she wouldn't consider qualified to pass such a judgement, would never in the world be able to influence her.

As for Esparza . . . He stopped digging the little trench. *There* was a man whose judgement she respected. If *Esparza* told her she couldn't act, she would believe him!

Fred went back to work, finished the ditching and stepped into the shade for a brief breather. He was still standing there, leaning upon the shovel, when Domingo came around to see how the trenching had gone. In a casual voice the stableman said, 'The car just drove in. I saw it from over in the pasture by the road. The three of them, again.'

Fred's eyes lifted. '*Three* of them?'

'Mister Spencer, Esparza and Jacqueline. Why; weren't all of them supposed to come down today?'

'Esparza wasn't.'

Domingo also stepped into the shade. 'Well, no one can say how things will turn out, eh? By the way, I went to the store this morning and brought back some of that special beer. Care for a bottle?'

Fred was hot and sweaty and would have indeed enjoyed a bottle, but if it had been one hour earlier or perhaps four hours later, not now.

Domingo departed to curry the pair of animals he'd brought in from the pasture while Fred went to put up the shovel at the tool-shed. Oddly, he felt a little tense, the way he had felt in former times when he'd been about to embark upon something that was dangerous.

There was no danger here, he told himself as he left the shed and headed for his quarters to put on a dry shirt and wash his hands and face. Even Nick Esparza, rumoured to be some kind of racketeer, could hardly be considered dangerous. At least not in the same league as some of the men Fred had gone up against elsewhere.

He decided the nervousness must come from the anticipated contact with the girl, not any of the men, and that was interesting, for although he had originally thought of her as very lovely and very desirable, after the trip to Chicago he had developed a different opinion of her. Not a very flattering one, so there was nothing like personal sentiment involved. Or was there?

He went back outside, squinted skyward to guess the time, thought it had to be a little after ten o'clock, then strolled over towards the stable courtyard, and didn't quite get there before movement off through the trees on his left caught and held his attention.

She was coming through the heat and shadows from the direction of the house with that graceful, long stride, and she was wearing jodhpurs and a loose white sweater. Her heavy mane of ash-blonde hair was caught back at the base of her head with a white ribbon. She looked like a very knowledgeable horsewoman, which he assumed she was.

She also looked very long-stemmed, full-busted and beautiful. He wondered what was really lacking to make her a qualified actress because as far as he could see, she most certainly had all the primary assets.

Domingo hissed from the courtyard and Fred turned. 'I tied your horse in his stall. I'll leave her horse outside in the shade of the courtyard. Now I'll go out in the pasture where the mares are. Good luck.'

Fred smiled. Domingo's face was shiny with nervous perspiration and his dark eyes were slitted with the expression of a conspirator. Then

Domingo pulled back and hastened away.

Fred went around into the courtyard but remained at the far end where he wouldn't be easily visible, and there he sat down upon a tackbox to wait. His heart was sturdily pounding, which was ridiculous; what possible peril could be involved here?

Chapter Nine

A SHOCKER

She didn't see him until she'd untied the horse, had led it to a water-trough closer to where he was sitting. Then she surprised him by nodding as though there had never been any unpleasantness between them. She said, 'It is a hot day, Mister Nufall.'

He agreed, arose and strolled closer to lean upon a hitching-rack. 'It is that, Miss Spencer. Almost too hot for horseback riding.'

She watched the horse drink, then answered without looking up. 'Not really. In this kind of weather you just poke along for the pleasure of it. There are a lot of shady places.' Her eyes swept up and zeroed-in on him. 'Have you watered your horse, Mister Nufall?'

He knew at once something had gone wrong. 'Should I?' he asked.

'If you intend to go riding with me, I think you should.'

'I see. And — do I intend to ride with you, Miss Spencer?'

She didn't smile. Her study of him was hard and steady. 'Mister Nufall, there is a saddled horse tied in one of the stalls. You were sitting here obviously waiting for something when I arrived. And now I'm also wondering why my grandfather asked if I wouldn't like to exercise one of the animals, if he hadn't also arranged the rest of this.'

Fred sighed, straightened up and went after the cross-tied animal in the stall. *No need for taking this thing seriously,* he told himself, mockingly. *It's just a simple thing about a misguided girl!* He was smiling tightly down around the lips when he led the horse across to the trough. Jacqueline was already out in the centre of the courtyard tightening the girth. She turned and leaned across her horse's back from the off-side watching him.

He grinned at her. 'You skunked me, lady.'

She smiled for the first time. 'It wasn't very hard. But it *was* disillusioning. I thought surely someone with all your cloak-and-dagger experience would be much more clever.'

He knew she'd been asking her father about him. But there was nothing to say, so he simply swore to himself and went right on smiling at her.

She finished with her animal then waited for him to cinch up. He watched how gracefully she mounted, and dragged himself up into the saddle.

'Where away?' she asked, letting him come abreast of her.

'You know the land, I don't.'

She didn't tighten her knees nor lift the reins.

'Mister Nufall, if I asked you point-blank what my grandfather is up to, would you tell me?'

'You want a point-blank answer?'

'Yes.'

He shook his head at her. 'No.'

She smiled again, but it was that annoyed, strained smile. She urged her horse out and they left the stable courtyard, rode at once out into shimmering heat, then she set their course for a grove of distant oaks and took down a deep breath and tipped her face to the faded, flawless blue sky.

'Sometimes it's enough just to be alive, isn't it?' he said.

She didn't answer, didn't even lower her face nor act as though he were there beside her.

The horses, water-loggy, walked without enthusiasm, which was fine with Fred whose riding ability was limited to a good sense of balance and little else.

Up ahead some animals in pasture saw the riders and ran up to the fence to stand and stare, heads up, tails out. He started to comment about that because the horses would have made an excellent picture, then checked himself. She had made it painfully plain the last time he'd spoken that she was through considering him her companion.

Still, he admired the way those curious horses stood and stared, and a little later, as they moved along towards the grove of trees she'd set their course for, he saw a flash of blue-grey, and a deer broke cover and fled from their approach.

'Wonderful,' he said quietly. 'It must have been a fascinating world before people started cluttering it up.'

She continued to ride at his side looking straight ahead, but he saw her eye flicker at sight of the deer, so she must have thought it graceful too. At least he wanted to believe she would see beauty there.

Suddenly she said, 'The only people who really clutter up this world, Mister Nufall, are the meddlers. The incorrigible, inveterate meddlers.'

He sighed. 'Me, of course.'

'You.'

They rode all the way to the grove before he spoke again. 'Tell me something about yourself, Miss Spencer: What is the point in trying to become something you don't really have to become.'

She looked at him just as they passed through the first shady place. 'What do you know about what I want to become?'

'I've seen your act. I've also listened to people talk about this Broadway play Esparza is backing for you.'

'All right. What of it?'

'Why do you want to be an actress?'

She hauled back, stopping her horse. 'Why do you want to be whatever it is you want to be, Mister Nufall? Why does anyone want to accomplish something?'

'But — an actress.'

'You're not that old-fashioned. The acting arts are just as respectable nowadays as — well — medicine, or something like that.'

Of course he could have disputed her simile, but he didn't because he hadn't meant his statement as she had interpreted it. 'You read me wrong, Miss Spencer. You're something special. You don't have to deal in your figure to make it in this world. What I meant was, why do you really want to be an actress when you could be doing really great and important things. Like working with handicapped kids, or —'

'You never impressed me as a missionary-type, Mister Nufall.'

He watched her dismount and lead her horse farther into the coolness of the oak grove, and after a moment he followed after her, leading his horse too.

'You didn't answer the question,' he said, and she stopped, whirled, and he saw the anger moving in the dark-granite depths of her eyes.

'I don't have to answer your question, Mister Nufall!'

His wish had been to make her angry and he had succeeded, The rest of the strategy was to make her furious enough to spit defiance at him.

But he didn't do it. He smiled and said, 'That's right, you don't. I'm the gardener.'

'Stop it,' she said hurling the words at him. 'You're no more a gardener than I am. I'll tell you what I think, Mister Nufall: My grandfather hired you for some special purpose. Some cloak-and-dagger scheme he's hatched, and it probably involves me. Probably it also involves my fiancé. Well, Mister Nufall, be careful. Nick isn't someone to be toyed with.'

'Nick doesn't concern me,' he retorted. 'And your grandfather hired me as his gardener. Nothing more. Your father did the actual hiring and you can't believe, if there was a plot, he'd be in on it, can you?'

She made a little gesture as she replied. 'My father couldn't care less. But Mister Nufall, my father was very impressed by your past record, both as a soldier and as a kind of hired troubleshooter. Would you like to know why I've wanted to see you again?'

He nodded, surprised that she'd wanted to.

'Because I can't figure you out. You've made a lot of money taking chances in the Middle-East, and elsewhere. Then you show up here as a gardener making a pittance each month.'

He stood gazing at her a moment, then he said, 'Do you really want to know why?'

'Yes.'

He motioned. 'Then sit down there in the grass.' She sat, letting the reins drop, permitting the horse to move off to graze. 'Now make a fair trade and I'll tell you.'

She nodded. 'I thought that was coming. All right, I'll answer your question. I want to be a successful actress because I've never been a success at anything, and even my father didn't even know I was alive all the time I was growing up. Is that enough for you?'

He turned his animal loose too, dropped down in the shady grove at her side, then shook his head. 'Miss Spencer, you just aren't that shallow. Okay; you've been neglected. Maybe you used to cry yourself to sleep at boarding-school, but now you're a woman. The scars may still be there, deep down, but the pain isn't.' He looked over at her. 'You aren't the kind of person who drives themselves hard just to be avenged.'

'Mister Freud,' she said drily, 'you could be very wrong.'

He kept watching her, and after a bit he sighed and leaned back against a tree. 'Lady, if you knew how many uprooted recruits and hard-drinking old-timers I've sat up with over the years, you'd give me a little more credit for knowing people.'

'Women?'

That was a bull's-eye. 'Not women, no. But you're not just women; you are a special woman. I won't believe you're that spiteful and vicious.'

'Thanks,' she said, and tugged at a blade of grass. 'It's my money,' she murmured.

He blinked. 'You're kidding.'

'No. I wish I were. Do you remember when you saw me looking like I was going to cry in the courtyard of the stable? Well; that was why.'

'Let me understand this. It's your money that is financing that show at the Tivoli?'

'No, not that show. The one to be put on in

New York. The Tivoli is owned in part by Nick. After we started dating he put me into that show. Then he said I should be on Broadway.'

Fred groaned. 'You can't be that dumb.'

She shot him a dark look. 'Oh no? Well, have you ever failed at everything, then had someone build up your ego until you really believed everything they told you?'

He didn't answer. This wasn't at all the way he'd planned for their meeting to progress. By now she should have been so enraged she'd be shouting things at him, or at least shouting enough of the truth for him to figure the rest of it out. But there she sat looking about as she'd looked the first time he'd ever spoken to her, and instead of feeling bitterly superior towards her, he was sitting there feeling terribly sorry for her, and very indignant towards Esparza.

He said, 'Are you going through with it?'

'That, Mister Nufall, is the problem. Nick's been telling me for a year how good I am. But I also get the reviews and he seems to be the only one who thinks I'm good at all.' She flung the blade of grass away. 'A few times one particular reviewer said I had promise. I found out he was on Nick's payroll.'

'Lady; you're going to marry this man?'

She started to jump to her feet but he caught her arm and held her down. 'Answer me.'

She struggled but only briefly, then she flung up her head and said, 'Why don't you leave it right there? What will you do now, go tell my grandfather? Of course I'm going to marry him. I have to.'

'Why?'

'Because when my money was gone I signed notes and now he holds them. If I don't marry him he is going to sue my father. Have you any idea what that kind of a scandal will do to the Spencer reputation, not to mention the companies and banks my father directs?'

He let go of her arm. 'But how will marrying him help?'

'My wedding present will be the notes.'

'Okay; and after that?'

'I — don't know. I suppose I'll be his wife until he doesn't need me any more.' She looked away. 'Pretty, isn't it?'

'No,' he said, 'it's stupid. You are stupid. Dumb as they come.'

She whirled, arm raised, face as white as a sheet. He caught the arm long before the blow fell, forced it down and said, 'One more answer then you can swing to your heart's desire: Do you really think you can act?'

'No.'

He released her arm. 'Now you listen to me. I'm not going to tell your grandfather the worst part of this. I'll have to tell him something, because he'll ask. But the worst of it will be just between you and me. Unless you run to Esparza and tell him I'm involved.'

'Why would I do that?'

He stood up, caught her and pulled her up too,

then he retained his hold of her shoulders. 'Because you're some kind of very special idiot, maybe. As for Esparza, you keep up the act with him.'

'What are you going to do, Mister Nufall?'

'Think for a day or two. Then move. That's all you've got to know. Now let's get mounted and get back. To start with I don't want your father and Esparza to start wondering about us both being gone at the same time.'

'Mister Nufall, I —'

'Shut up and get on the damned horse!'

Chapter Ten

A WET NIGHT

When they got back to the stable he was still angry and she was not. Later, that would come back to him as a special irony; it was supposed to be the other way around.

But right then he wasn't thinking of her. As they dismounted he jerked his head at her. 'Go on back to the house. Wash your face in cold water. That may help. Then go on in with the others and be yourself.'

She stood looking at him but he took the reins to her horse and marched away, leaving her alone. She finally turned and left the stable courtyard.

He had the horses unsaddled when Domingo arrived, looking suspiciously cool and dry for someone who supposedly had been working out in one of the pastures. Domingo took over the off-bridling.

'She got mad at you,' said Salazar, fishing for information.

Fred shot a look at the stableman that was a little bleak and unfriendly, then he went over to the trough, doused his face and head, let water trickle down inside his shirt, and afterwards he shook his head and said, 'Not as mad as she did that other time.'

Domingo was pleased. As he stalled the horses across the courtyard he called back over his shoulder that although he hadn't been spying on them, he had seen which way they'd ridden. Then, returning from the last stall, he said, 'You know, after seeing her ride so many years, I could tell that this time she wasn't feeling very happy. Maybe that was it; she was demoralized.'

Fred leaned beside the trough letting the water dry to cool him. 'Maybe,' he replied. 'How about the others at the house? Did you just happen to have one eye on them too?'

Domingo trudged over looking properly pained. 'Of course not. I don't eavesdrop on people. But anyway, they sat out on the loggia drinking iced highballs.'

Fred grinned. There was no way to see the front loggia and the oak grove from the same position. Domingo had to see first which way he and Jacqueline went, then he would have had to slip around to the north side of the mansion to see the three men on the loggia.

He straightened up off the rack beside the trough. 'Does that offer of a cold beer still hold?'

Domingo's face creased into a wide, dark smile. 'Come along.'

There had been clouds accumulating over along the easterly horizon for some time now. Domingo had been watching them but Fred hadn't. Domingo's interest was personal; if it rained he would not have to use the overhead irrigation system, which involved considerable physical activity on a very hot day.

A little wind sprang up, which was the first thing to call Fred's attention to the weather. He was standing out front with Domingo, beneath the wide overhang out front of the barn when the little wind went galloping across the shingles.

Domingo, wiping beer-foam from his lips, nodded approvingly. 'Pretty soon now it will rain.'

He was right. The first drops began falling about a half-hour later. They seemed to be fat, heavy, and wide-spaced, but by the time another half-hour had passed the torrent was coming straight down, the little wind was gone, and everywhere people stood beneath roofs it sounded like a constant roll of huge drums.

There was little work to be done in that weather, although Domingo could scamper from stall to stall without too much peril, to feed horses, and after he'd got his slicker on he went tramping down to the goat-house to herd all the kittens, and their mother, inside, and close the door.

Fred sat in one of the spring-back steel chairs out front of his quarters, smoking his pipe, the perfect picture of relaxation, unless one got close enough to observe the expression on his face. Then he still looked relaxed, but in a different way; relaxed the way a cougar looks while crouching on a limb over a sleeping calf.

The downpour continued unabated for more than one hour, which wasn't unusual. It diminished somewhat during the second hour, which was also typical of an Illinois summer thundershower.

Finally, just before the sun would have dropped away, if it had been visible through the darkly lowering storm-clouds, the drops, still large, came only very infrequently, and except for the steady dripping of trees and drain-pipes, the silence was as before.

Only a little while later Erin Clancy rang the dinner bell. Fred waited out front for Domingo, then they went across to the main house together, which they usually did.

Erin Clancy gave Fred an odd look when he and Domingo entered her kitchen, but if the look had any significance he was sure he couldn't guess what it was, and she said nothing that would offer a clue, so he shrugged it off and went ahead to eat his dinner.

Afterwards, when Domingo was already out back waiting, Erin came forward to intercept Fred with a stealthy glide and said, 'Mister Spencer's waitin' t'see ya in the study.'

He leaned down and said, 'Fine, love. Now tell me where the study is.'

She stepped back, gave him a dark look, then proceeded to lead the way out into the large formal dining-room and point from the archway that separated dining-hall from sitting-room.

'That carved door on across the parlour. Just

knock, then walk on in.'

She turned before he could thank her, and went back into her kitchen.

Fred crossed the parlour, was impressed by its elegance, its somewhat old-fashioned but splendid permanence, and rapped upon the carved door. Merritt Spencer opened it and stood aside for Fred to enter. Upon the desk were two great brandy beakers with a spot of excellent tobacco-coloured liquor in each one. Having been refused once, Merritt left his guest no chance for a second refusal. He handed Fred a glass and said, 'I'd have come down, but that confounded rain was a fright.' Merritt's searching gaze remained upon Fred's face. His eyes, faded somewhat now, had at one time been the same unique gunmetal-blue colour as were his granddaughter's eyes. 'Well?' he said, a trifle testily.

Fred'd had that quiet time during the rainstorm to complete his earlier uncharitable thoughts. Now he said, 'I think I'll handle this my own way. Mister Spencer.'

The older man looked shocked. 'What do you mean? This is my affair, not yours!'

'Well maybe, Mister Spencer, but it's beginning to grow into something unpleasant.'

'Explain that!'

Fred sipped the brandy then put the beaker upon the desk behind Merritt Spencer. 'She means to marry Esparza, but it's just not all that simple. As far as he is concerned . . .'

'Yes?'

'He's after her for what she can do for him socially.'

'You've already told me that.'

Fred nodded. 'And that's about all I'm going to tell you, too.'

They stood fifteen feet apart with Merritt's eyes darkening with anger. Finally he said, 'Fred, don't bother sparing my feelings. They've had some pretty rough bruises this past year or so. Don't be gallant, man. If you think something needs doing, and doubt my ability to stomach it, let me disabuse you on that score.'

Fred grinned when he hadn't meant to, but that one word was so old-fashioned; it told all anyone had to know about Merritt Spencer's ability to handle someone like Nick Esparza.

'Let me put it this way, Mister Spencer: I've been this route before. Granted, you have a right to know things, I won't keep them from you — afterwards.'

'Fred, I don't like the sound of that. If Jacqueline is in some kind of serious difficulty, I have an attorney who can —'

'I'm sure he can, sir, and I also anticipate that he may have to, before we're through. But for now I'd appreciate it if you'd show the kind of trust you did when we discussed my going up to the city.'

Merritt screwed up his face. 'But if you're thinking in terms of violence, Fred, you've simply got to understand we just can't have anything like that.'

'I understand, Mister Spencer.' Fred edged backwards a little, towards the door.

Spencer halted him. 'Confound it, man, you're making this seem awfully conspiratorial and under-handed. All I wanted to know was whether my granddaughter is —'

'I know what you wanted, Mister Spencer, and I've told you she plans to go through with that marriage. I can also tell you she intends to go on to Broadway. But she doesn't really want to do that Broadway show. Not any more.'

'You're not making any sense.'

Fred, the doorknob in his grip behind his back, smiled. 'I know I'm not. I'll see you in the morning, Mister Spencer.'

He got out of the study and across the sitting-room before Merritt Spencer emerged in the doorway still holding his brandy snifter and looking thunderous. It hadn't been a very successful interview for either of them, but it *had* left Merritt Spencer with a bad premonition.

As far as Fred was concerned, when he went hiking back through the darkness he was disgusted with himself for botching it that way. His intention had been to simply gloss things over, reiterate what Merritt Spencer already knew. But the older man had driven too suddenly and too fiercely to the point. He had managed to drive past Fred's defences too suddenly and too completely.

Still though, Fred had no intention of telling Spencer what he had in mind. He didn't intend telling anyone, and although Domingo's door was open to let in the cool night air, which was an invitation for Fred to stop in and perhaps view television with Salazar for a bit, he slipped right on past.

Later, he left the estate on foot for the two mile trek to the nearest village, a crossroads place called Wayne, and there, at a smoky and rather noisy tavern he fished out a small address book, and using it as a reference, made six telephone calls, each of them a toll-call. In fact, he ran out of change and had to get more from a barman before completing his final call.

After that he paused to have a cold beer at the little bar, to sit and softly smile while he recapitulated what had been said, very profanely, among the three men he'd been able to contact out of the six he had called, then he started back to the estate.

Halfway the clouds opened up again. It hadn't occurred to him that this might happen so he'd neglected to wear his raincoat. In fact, he hadn't even put on a jacket.

By the time he got back to his quarters he was soaked to the skin. But he still felt good, so after a warm shower and a change of clothing, he went outside in the lonely night to have a final smoke before retiring.

There was a light over at the mansion. He watched it, thinking how he'd caused Merritt Spencer all that anxiety.

But if Merritt Spencer knew where his gardener had been or the gist of those tough-voiced and profane conversations he'd been involved in, Merritt Spencer would have had more reason than ever for anxiety.

The rain started again, continued for perhaps fifteen minutes, then stopped. Fred arose, knocked out his pipe, went indoors, leaving the front door open to catch the breeze.

He slept like a baby that night, arose early, as was his habit, and was down feeding the cats when Domingo came hiking along in response to Erin's breakfast bell. Salazar said, 'You sure got in late last night.'

Fred arose, closed the gate to the goat-pen, grinned and fell in beside Salazar. 'You know, Domingo, you would make someone a good wife — you nag enough for it.'

Domingo looked briefly indignant, then he gave his shoulders a great shrug and, ramming both hands into his trouser pockets trudged along almost to the mansion before speaking again.

'Okay. Just remember, though. If you don't want to tell me what is going on, that's all right. Only you are getting in up to your neck, just like I predicted.'

Fred held the kitchen door for Salazar to pass in first, and only smiled. Erin Clancy saw that smile, thought it had been meant for her, and smiled back. Evidently she had recovered from her mild pique of the evening before.

Chapter Eleven

A CURIOUS DAY

Except for Merritt Spencer's visit to the rose garden where Fred worked the next morning, there was nothing extraordinary about this day until late in the afternoon.

Those roses, which formed a large crescent around a delightful little stone arbour with benches, needed pruning, and the ground needed mulching. Fred had already pruned them and was doing the mulching, when Merritt Spencer came along puffing on a pipe that had a big, droopy curve to it, and wearing a houndstooth-check plaid jacket.

There were oaks, elms, and several varieties of flowering trees nearby to make it shady around the arbour, although after the thundershower of the day before it was not hot. Humid and cool, instead, although the heat would come later.

Mulching was good exercise. At least that was what old Merritt said as he stopped in the sunshine for a moment to watch Fred work.

He mentioned the pleasant morning, too, and how much penetration there had been after the rainfall. He did not mention his granddaughter, nor in any way act as though he were any more than the master of the estate passing a little idle time with his gardener.

Fred shot the older man a sceptical look once or twice, but went along with the charade. The mulching, he said, could best be done when the ground was soft, and it helped too that the weather was cool enough so that it was possible to work out in it.

Merritt puffed and nodded, then stepped over into the shade of the arbour and sat upon one of the benches, legs crossed. 'Roses require a good deal of care,' he said. 'Actually, they are a very hardy plant. I've seen them revert to a native state in unkempt gardens, and they do very well. The biggest problem with them is bugs. Do you agree?'

Fred nodded without looking up. 'Bugs,' he repeated.

Merritt removed the pipe, peered into the bowl, then leaned to knock the dottle into the rose bed. 'The unfortunate part of that, of course, is the rose's inability to take care of itself.'

Fred stopped working and leaned on his shovel eyeing the older man. 'Allegory, Mister Spencer?'

'Well, you must admit that no matter how hardy a rose is, Fred, they don't know everything. Some kind of strategy has to be devised to protect them from the bugs, eh?'

Fred had a hunch about this and didn't like it. 'Mister Spencer, are you implying that you are taking some kind of steps to protect Jacqueline?'

'As a matter of fact, Fred, I spoke to my attorney this morning.'

'What could you tell him? She is her own boss, and she says she intends to marry Esparza. If you butt in she's going to be pretty damned angry with you. Also, I have a feeling Esparza isn't much afraid of lawyers. Not many people are who own one or two of them.'

'I'm not butting in, and it wasn't entirely of her that we spoke. I also mentioned you.'

Fred continued to lean and say nothing.

'After our discussion last night it appeared to me you were devising some scheme of your own. Probably something physical. I wanted Mister Logan to be prepared for whatever unpleasantness might ensue. In other words, what we discussed had to do with his schedule for the next week or so — I presume your scheme will be in progress by that time?'

Fred still leaned, eyeing his employer. After a bit he said, 'You didn't by any chance also call your son, or granddaughter?'

'Of course not.'

Fred resumed his work and for a while neither of them said anything. It began to turn hot. The humidity was already high so the heat made any kind of physical labour that much more difficult.

Eventually Merritt said, 'Would you be interested in hearing what I think?'

Fred paused again. He was nearing the end of the mulching. 'Shoot. You're the boss here.'

'I think that somehow you and my granddaughter didn't fight this time; that you somehow coaxed her into telling you something shocking, and that your natural reaction was one of indignation towards Esparza. But, because you wished to spare me involvement in violence, you have chosen to deal me out, so to speak, and deal yourself in.'

'So you alerted your attorney to be ready to bail me out.'

'Well, not exactly, but something like that. At least to keep himself free to move instantly if there is any trouble.'

'Mister Spencer, I'm not going to leave this estate. Now how can I be involved in anything violent if I stay right here?'

Merritt smiled. 'I have no idea, Fred. On the other hand, the little I know of your past inclines me to believe that somehow or other, you'll manage.' He arose from the bench, for although it was shady in there, the heat was able to penetrate without any trouble. He took off his coat and draped it over one shoulder. 'The thing I'm most interested in, Fred, is what my granddaughter told you.'

'Mister Spencer, you don't expect me to violate a confidence do you?'

Spencer considered that a moment, then gently smiled. 'Of course not. Gentlemen just don't do things like that. However, without violating any confidence, you might suggest some course for Jay Logan, the attorney, to be prepared to pursue.'

'I doubt very much if Mister Logan will be needed. As I just said, Mister Spencer, I'll be right here on the estate.'

Merritt had to give up. Anyway, it was getting along towards midday and the heat out there was becoming almost unpleasant, what with all that moisture still in the atmosphere. He lingered a little longer, back again on the topic of roses, then went ambling off in the direction of the mansion.

Fred watched him go, then shook his head and went back to work. He finished the mulching, then went to his quarters for a shower, and by the time he'd finished with that Erin Clancy rang the bell for their noon-day meal.

Domingo appeared looking wilted and sweaty. Fred agreed to wait for him, and leaned upon the railing outside Salazar's quarters until Domingo had washed up and had made himself presentable. If he hadn't, Erin Clancy would probably have given him a piece of her mind. She was not the type to tolerate sweaty and unwashed people in her kitchen.

Fred did not mention his talk with Merritt Spencer and evidently Domingo had not known any such meeting had taken place because he made none of his usual little leading remarks.

In fact, the luncheon passed off without any more than the usual small-talk and afterwards, when Fred and Salazar were heading back towards the stable-area, Domingo holding a tin of condensed milk he'd wangled away from Erin Clancy for his thriving horde of cats, he said it almost seemed as though life were back where it used to be before all this trouble with Jacqueline Spencer disrupted things.

Fred simply smiled.

The little kittens still had their eyes closed, but otherwise they were fat and furry and continually complaining. The mother-cat was grateful for the milk, and when one of her obnoxious offspring fell into the dish she cuffed it out with exasperated severity.

Domingo went to put the tin of milk, what remained of it, in a cooler. Fred went to the tool shed for some shears, then headed for the flowering thicket north of the house where a hydrangea tree grew amid some bushes of the same name that climbed a low rock wall spilling colour wherever they touched.

Whatever people did for the balance of this day, should be done at a leisurely pace and in shade. The combined heat and humidity made movement an effort.

Fred, in excellent physical shape, did not rush at his work. There was no need in any case. By now he had the area around the building fairly well under control. Farther out across the fields there was considerable pruning and general maintenance to be done, but there was no hurry about it.

He, in fact, worked around the hydrangea perimeter until he saw a car hasten past and turn in down at the front gate. It was a convertible vehicle and even with the silk *babushka* to keep her hair from flying, and the enormous eye-shades, Fred recognized Jacqueline Spencer.

He straightened up back there in the shade, hooked his shears in a tree-limb, then felt through his pockets for pipe and tobacco. By the time she reached the parkway out front of the house he was ready to light up. But he held off for a moment, until he'd had a chance to see her get out of the car.

She didn't step out, she sprang out, and she didn't stroll up to the steps and across the marble loggia, she practically flew.

Fred lit his pipe, said, 'Oh, oh,' aloud to himself, and reached up to reclaim the shears as he headed back towards the tool shed. 'She's mad as a wet hen.'

He put the tools away, went over into the courtyard of the stable, found a bamboo rake he'd seen Domingo use to keep the gravel courtyard and the tanbark edges neat, and went to work raking. It was neither his area of responsibility, nor his kind of work, but he had a fair idea that when the female-hurricane arrived, it would descend upon him in the courtyard because that was usually where they met.

Domingo came first, though, stood watching Fred work for a moment, then vigorously scratched his curly, dark head, stepped forth where Fred could see him and said, 'Hey; don't you have enough of your own work to do?'

Fred smiled. 'Domingo, I am expecting a female commando to step in here and cut me down any minute, and I'd prefer killing the time while I'm waiting being busy.'

Domingo's eyes widened. 'Her — again — here?'

'Yes. Any minute now.'

'Mad again too?'

'Very mad.'

Domingo rolled up his eyes, raised his hands in abject supplication, then glided soundlessly back around the corner of the stable and disappeared.

Fred stopped raking, stepped over to an archway leading from the stable courtyard around to the northerly end of the building where the hired-men lived, and in that cool archway had an excellent sighting up across the intervening distance towards the main house.

He actually anticipated seeing her come across from that direction with pleasure, for angry or not, she was very pleasant to watch in motion.

But as far as he could see, through shadows and sunshine, there was no movement. He frowned. It was quite impossible that she was up there letting off steam at her grandfather. He had not been sure whether she would do that or not. After all, she and Fred *did* have a kind of pact.

Maybe she wasn't doing that, but nonetheless she'd been very angry when she'd arrived, so she was in there saying *something*.

Finally, Fred saw her, and at once the reason

for the long interval of waiting was clear. She had changed from the linen suit she'd been wearing when she walked across the loggia, into jodhpurs and a beige blouse, to go horseback riding.

He groaned, put aside the rake and leaned in the shade thinking that of all the things he did not especially desire to do on a day as hot as this one was, was going horseback riding.

She passed from the shade into the sunshine. There was an expanse of several acres between the house-area where great trees provided shade, and measure of seclusion, and the stable-area, where more trees grew, that was open grassland.

She strode along as though the heat were not oppressive. He admired that, because while he was not particularly averse to heat himself, heat *and* humidity were something else. But she didn't even seem to notice.

He let her get almost completely across the shadeless place, then sauntered forth to stand in the archway in plain sight. She did not see him at once, but eventually she did, and veered off at once to head directly for him.

He watched, and bleakly smiled to himself. She wasn't sauntering with the grace of a lovely woman this time, she was bearing down upon him like a marching battalion.

Chapter Twelve

AN EAVESDROPPER

He stepped back so she could enter the archway, then he turned to pass along back towards the courtyard. She said nothing, no greeting, no outburst, not a sound until they were in the seclusion of the courtyard, with horse-stalls and tack, feed, and hay rooms on three sides of them. The only open area was southward, where the squared horseshoe of the stable offered a pleasant vista of turf, and, more distantly, trees.

'Deny it,' she said, controlling her voice to keep it low. 'Just say you had nothing to do with it!'

He leaned upon the blanket-rack eyeing her very placidly, 'All right, if you wish, I'll deny it.'

'Liar!' she hurled at him.

He sighed. 'Lady; there are no rules to this game, so we'll have to make them up as we go along. I can pretend I don't know what you are talking about, but since you've already called me a liar on that score, I guess being stubborn wouldn't help us any. So — all right, I knew it would happen.'

'Knew it would happen! You had no right to do that at all. And if you think I won't say anything about it —'

'Just tell me this: While you were in the house, did you tell your grandfather anything?'

'I should have! I most certainly should have told him — but I didn't. And I haven't told Nick about you either. Not yet anyway.'

'Lady; you don't like Nick, remember?'

'That's the truth! And after what you did to him this morning I classify you in the same category.'

'I haven't left this estate all day. Ask your grandfather; ask Domingo or Erin Clancy.'

She glared. 'I didn't say you *personally,* were with those men who paid a call on Nick at his penthouse. Mister Nufall, I underestimated you before, but I've made a correction. You are ruthless, cruel, savage, and . . .'

'No gentleman?'

'Don't try to be amusing!'

He shrugged. 'How did you know anything happened to Mister Esparza?'

'I telephoned, and he told me. You are lucky — so far, at any rate — because he thinks it was someone else.'

'Who else?'

'I don't know. He didn't say. And what did you expect to accomplish by having him beaten up?'

Fred kept gazing at her. 'Is that what they did? I thought it would be just a little mugging. Nothing really too rough.'

'I don't believe you. I know about your background, and —'

'I'm getting tired of hearing people say they know about my background. I was never a hoodlum nor a racketeer. As for Esparza getting a few lumps, I didn't know it would amount to much.'

'Well; he had three friends with him. They started to fight.'

Fred smiled. 'Oh; well of course that *would* make a difference. I have a feeling that those three gentlemen who paid Mister Esparza a call were not the kind of people who like it when other people start heaving their weight around.'

Jacqueline glared at him. 'Who were they?'

'Why; so you can tell Esparza?'

'Have I told anyone yet about any of this?'

'I don't know; have you?'

'Of course not. I realized — until this morning at any rate — that you were trying to help me. We were — allies. But, Mister Nufall, after what happened at the penthouse this morning I'm not going to let you —'

'Wait a minute,' said Fred, and looked around for a chair, found one nearby and pointed to it. 'Sit down in the shade.'

'I don't want to sit down.'

'*Sit — down!*'

She moved over very obediently and sat down. He smiled at her. 'Now just tell me one thing, Jacqueline: Do you, or do you not, care for Esparza?'

'I don't. And I've already told you that. But what kind of a person do you think I am; I'm not going to sit idly by while some gangsters —'

'Not gangsters, and I've already explained that to you.'

'Excuse me — not gangsters. Just hoodlum roughnecks. And I can't just sit by and watch you use this kind of violence.'

'Do you want to marry him?'

'No!'

'Are you going to marry him the fifteenth of next month?'

'No!'

'And, lady, what do you think he is going to say — and probably do — when you tell him that? Do you imagine for a moment a man like Nick Esparza cares a tinker's damn about your grandfather's lawyer, or about some remonstrance you might make?'

'You can't just have him beaten up.'

Fred smiled at her without one whit of humour. 'He wasn't beaten up. Roughed-up a little, maybe, but even that wouldn't have happened if he hadn't tried to throw his weight around. And those men who called on him — three of them — they aren't hoodlums or gangsters. They've been trained to eat gangsters for breakfast. They are old associates of mine.'

'But what can such a thing possibly accomplish, Mister Nufall? You can't just go around knocking people into agreeing with you.'

'I don't intend to. And as far as Esparza is concerned, what happened will be a mystery to him for a couple of days. When I get around to it, he'll know why it happened. But not until I get around to it. Now — as for you — when you ran into the house an hour ago, you were angry. Your grandfather is anything but a fool. Even if you didn't say anything to him, he'll suspect something, won't he?'

She bit her lip and held it for a moment gazing up at him as though she wanted to discuss the act of violence further, as though she thought she was being side-tracked, and would like to resist.

'Well?' he said sharply.

'No, I doubt that he suspected anything. Although I was tempted to say something. I didn't. I simply ran upstairs to my old room, when I stayed out here in the summers, changed to riding clothes, then came back down.'

'He wasn't waiting?' asked Fred, scowling about this.

She nodded. 'He was waiting. He wanted to know why I acted so upset. I told him the city was getting me down; that I had to drive out today and breathe some fresh air. It wasn't exactly a prevarication. I *did* need some fresh air.'

Fred leaned upon the blanket-rack with some of the earlier calmness, and smiled at her. 'But that won't fool him. Not Merritt Spencer.'

'If you tell him, Mister Nufall, he'll hit the ceiling. In our family we have never condoned violence for settling things.'

'No? Well it's a damned good thing for people like you *someone* believes it settles things — or you wouldn't be living the nice flat, soft, indulgent life right now!'

She started to retort, and colour climbed back to her face again, but he growled and made a slicing gesture that silenced her.

'Go saddle a horse,' he said, 'and take a ride.'

Her mouth dropped open. 'Don't you tell me what to do!'

He turned and looked steadily at her without speaking again. She arose, went over to the far row of stalls looking in each one. He watched her, neither offering to help, nor even to speak. But when she had a horse out and was saddling it, and glared across the animal's back at him, he smiled.

Domingo was correct. She needed being told.

'What are you looking so satisfied about?' she demanded.

'You, Miss Spencer. You may not have a lick of sense, but you're certainly lovely to look at.'

She made a kind of gutteral, strangling sound in her throat, yanked at the billets on the girth, and refused to look in his direction again.

He waited until she'd mounted, was urging the horse ahead towards the southward pass from the courtyard, then he turned and said, without raising his voice, 'You can come out now Domingo. Don't bother pretending you aren't hiding in the archway, because I saw your shadow.'

It wasn't Domingo. Merritt Spencer walked forth, and when Fred turned casually, still sardonically grinning, his employer said, 'Well; I forgot about shadows projecting out in front.'

Fred stared at the older man. Behind him Jacqueline was cantering off towards that distant oak grove where she and Fred had first hurled words back and forth without actually being angry at one another. At least not as angry as she had been on their first meeting.

Merritt fished out a pipe, rummaged his coat pockets, then looked up and said, 'What kind of tobacco do you smoke?'

Fred hesitated a moment before handing over his pouch. 'How long were you back there?' he finally asked.

Spencer proceeded to stuff his pipe-bowl without looking at Fred. 'Quite a while. I came down shortly after Jackie did. I wanted to know if you two had gone riding together. Well; you couldn't expect me to rush forth and denounce the pair of you, could you? And it was too interesting to turn and go back to the house. Do you by any chance have a match? I didn't come prepared at all, did I?'

Fred handed over his lighter. 'And . . . ?'

Merritt puffed up a head of smoke, killed the light and looked round for the chair his granddaughter had recently vacated. As he sat, he crossed one leg over the other one and very thinly smiled upwards.

'I don't know, to be truthful with you, Fred, I'll have to think it all over. I don't believe we've had anything like this happen before. But it might help if I knew *why* you had your friends go and —

visit — Mister Esparza.'

'You should get that from Jacqueline.'

'No; it's better man-to-man. Women cry a lot, or whimper, or get all upset. It was money, wasn't it?'

Fred said nothing. They kept looking directly at one another until Spencer removed the pipe and sighed with soft resignation.

'Maybe your way is best. It's certainly primitive and barbaric and very crude, though.'

'But it works, Mister Spencer, on some people. On a particular kind of person it's the only thing that *will* work.'

'How much money did she give him?'

'All she had, I think. Then she borrowed more and signed notes. And he bought up the notes. So now she marries him, gives him access to the Spencer-circles, or he sues your son, ruins her reputation, smears your son, and I suppose, smears you as well. Not very pretty is it?'

The old man didn't answer, but he bit savagely upon his pipestem, which could have been interpreted as a kind of answer, and his face turned very pale.

Fred heard a small sound, turned, saw Domingo entering the archway, caught Salazar's eye and gave his head an infinitesimal wag. Domingo got the signal, saw who was sitting in the chair, and without hardly shifting balance, turned on one foot and walked silently back out of sight again.

Merritt Spencer smoked and looked pale, kept

his eyes away from Fred, and finally switched position in the chair, crossing the other leg over its companion, then looked up and his face was set in harsh lines.

'How much did it cost to have your friends see Mister Esparza?'

'Their flight-fare to Chicago. None of them live close. And their incidental expenses. I suppose all told two thousand dollars.'

'I'll have it for you at dinner.' Merritt puffed, then said, 'What is your scheme; you didn't just have him manhandled for the joy of it?'

Fred straightened up and gave his head a dolorous shake. 'It would have been better if you'd stayed out of it.'

'Well, dammit, I didn't. So now you might as well tell me the rest of it.'

'All right. I'll let Mister Esparza worry for a few days, then I'll telephone him and suggest he cancel his engagement to your granddaughter, and mail those notes back to her. In return for which he will be reimbursed for the notes. And if he doesn't like that arrangement . . .'

'Yes? No, no; I don't want to hear it!' Merritt arose abruptly from the chair. 'Fred; I don't approve of your methods.' He cleared his throat, turned and went as far as the empty archway, then turned back and said, 'Will it cost another two thousand if they have to come back — these friends of yours — in case Mister Esparza becomes cantankerous?'

'I suppose so, yes.'

'Fine. I'll include that in the envelope that'll be beside your plate at dinner. Now — one more thing: Don't let my granddaughter know that I am aware of any of this.'

'Yes sir.'

'And Fred — wait until she comes back from the ride and help her unsaddle, will you?'

'Yes sir.'

Merritt Spencer walked quickly out through the archway and started across the turf back towards the house, smoke rising in little puffs in his wake.

Chapter Thirteen

JACQUELINE

Fred showered, changed to fresh sun-tans, and returned to the stable courtyard with a lighted pipe to keep him company. He didn't think about it, but he instinctively knew Domingo would appear, and he did, but entering the courtyard from the southward open end, which also happened to be the direction Jacqueline had ridden off in. Only in Domingo's case, he came from around to the left, which was the direction of the goat-pen.

Fred watched the stableman saunter towards him, and almost smiled as he remembered Domingo's two near-entrances and two equally as discreet withdrawals.

Domingo brought forth Fred's smile when he sighed, took a nearby chair and sank down into it as though he were completely exhausted. 'My friend, I can confide in you,' said Domingo unhappily. 'When the weather gets too steamy and uncomfortable, I have a cool place in the tack-room behind you where I can have a little *siesta*. But today I had to stay out of there.'

Fred laughed at the look of exaggerated pain on Salazar's face. 'Sorry about that,' he said. 'We were holding caucuses today.'

'You're going to get your hand in the wringer. I warned you.'

'I realize you are probably right. Now tell me — where were *you* eavesdropping?'

'Me?' asked Domingo, screwing up his face. 'Me, eavesdropping?' He shrugged. 'How could I do that, when the best place for it was already taken over by Mister Spencer? No; I stayed out in the north pasture.'

'The one with the big oaks in it?'

Domingo nodded. 'Yes. But it wasn't as pleasant as it would have been in the tack-room.'

A noise made them both look southward. Coming towards the stable at a slow canter was Jacqueline. She rode as though she were part of her horse. Domingo said, 'Here we go again,' and arose and started out of sight.

Fred stopped him. 'Take care of her horse, will you? I've got something to say to her.'

Domingo turned back, not very enthusiastically, and when she rode into the courtyard where he could see her expression, which was flinty and hard and aimed squarely at Fred Nufall, Domingo didn't utter a sound as he obediently went forward to be handed the reins as she stepped down.

She started past Fred towards the archway. He let her get just beyond him, then said, 'Your grandfather was here shortly after you went riding.'

She turned back, still silent, her eyes defiant,

her heavy mouth flattened a little in strong disapproval.

Fred went over to take her elbow and start her moving again. This time, although he thought Domingo would be occupied with the horse, and he was reasonably certain her grandfather was up at the manor-house, having heard enough for one day, he nevertheless steered her on through the archway, out across the overhang-area and past some flowerbeds to that wide, open expanse of turf where no one could possibly hear what they were saying.

When silence had run on too long she said, 'Well!'

He kept right on guiding her by the arm. 'Well; I suppose you are entitled to know the rest of it.'

'My grandfather?'

'Forget him. You're entitled to know what else I have in mind.'

'How awfully kind of you,' she murmured with acidy sarcasm.

He ignored that. 'If *you* had gone to Esparza and told him you were not going to marry him.' Fred looked around at her, finally, shrugging his shoulders, 'It might get a little nasty.'

'Do you think it won't if you butt in?'

His smile was flat and humourless. 'It may, for me. It may. But I've had a little more experience along these lines than you've had, I think. Anyway, you are going to act the part of his fiancé.'

'You think I'm a very poor actress.'

'Yes, that's a fact. But this role you'll be able to handle because you've already been doing it. And it's convinced him. Probably because he doesn't really give a damn whether you're fond of him or not; probably because he knows you're not and couldn't care less as long as you go through with the marriage. So — you act natural. You can even sympathize with him over his recent discomfort, if you like.'

'And meanwhile, back at the ranch . . .'

He laughed quietly. 'Right. Meanwhile I am going to convince *him* to break the engagement with *you*.'

'Just like that?'

'Well; of course that'll be up to him.'

'I see. And if he resists, then your friends pay him another call.'

'No. Next time I do it myself.'

'Fred, you're out of your mind. Nick just isn't the kind to be intimidated. Furthermore, the minute he realizes the pressure is on him to let me go, he's going to think my father or grandfather is behind it, and he'll strike back at them.'

'I've taken that into consideration. I've also taken into consideration the fact that he may even suspect you, after he knows what it's all about, of having him worked over.'

'I see. And your friends are standing by?'

He shook his head. 'No. They've gone back to their homes. I'll take care of it from here on. But what I want you to do is get your father to come out here over the week-end with you. That way, if

Esparza comes calling after he knows what's really at stake, he'll be here on the estate.'

'Where you can attack him?'

'For gosh sakes, Jacqueline, you've been watching too many thrillers on television. I'm not going to attack anyone.'

They were nearing the grove of trees that separated the stables from the mansion on ahead. It was shady, almost gloomy, in there, where huge old bowl-shaped treetops filtered out most of the sunlight in broad daylight, but now, in early evening, with little sunlight left, where the soft light of pre-gloaming lay in even, cool layers.

She stopped when they had entered the grove, turned and said, 'I don't want you to do this.'

He heard the different sound of her voice. She wasn't angry, she wasn't even annoyed. He guessed her new mood and might have responded but she gave him no choice, right then.

'You've already done enough. No, I don't mean that the way it sounded — as though you've interfered. I meant that you've tried to help and got yourself in danger when it wasn't your fight.'

He stood for a moment watching the way shadows touched her lovely face, the way they softened, lightened the colour of her hair, and made her golden-tan throat darker than it really was. Then he raised both hands, took her face in them, leaned down and kissed her very gently.

She stiffened, just for a moment, but when he neither bore down upon her mouth nor moved his hands, she loosened.

He drew back, dropped his hands and forced a little crooked grin. 'Hell of an affront — the yardman kissing the master's granddaughter. Well; this time I won't block it if you want to take a swing at me.'

She blushed, but otherwise did not lower her eyes nor step back. 'You were entitled to that,' she said quietly.

His grin winked out. 'Don't do me any favours, lady.'

She bit her lip, teetered there upon the edge of some kind of decision, then raised *her* hands to *his* face, drew him down and kissed *him*. It was a gentle, sweet kiss, the kind that though a man lived to be a hundred and experienced hundreds of kisses afterwards, would always stand out in his memory.

'Why do you always have to put the wrong interpretation on what I say?' she asked, afterwards.

He blew out a big breath, looked around, looked back, then leaned his back upon a rough-barked tree and said, 'I don't know. Is that what I do?'

'Yes. And you're terrible overbearing, at times.'

'I'll tell you something, Jacqueline . . .'

'What?'

'I'm almost ashamed to say it. I'm in love with you.' He paused, but only very briefly, then hurried his words. 'It wasn't for your grandfather, if that's why you think I butted into your private life. Well; at first, maybe, but not lately.'

She turned and went over where there was a distant view of the stables. He saw something catch her attention and also turned. Domingo was over there at the goat-pen feeding his brood of cats.

As though nothing was between them, there in the softness of the grove, she said, 'What is he doing?'

Fred explained about the cat and her kittens. At once Jacqueline's eyes brightened, she smiled tenderly. 'I didn't know. Can we go see them?'

He pushed off the tree. 'Sure. Right now?'

She turned when he came close, raised both her arms and caught him by the shoulders. 'I'll let you in on a secret. I rode back to the place where we went riding the other day, and I wished with all my might I'd never met you, that my grandfather had never hired you, and that you would go away — because you did something to me that I didn't believe any man could ever do.'

She tugged at him with wilful insistence.

Afterwards, when he'd let his hands drop away from her waist and she'd let go of his shoulders, he said, 'You can't mean it.'

She nodded in agreement. 'I know that. I don't want to mean it, either. Between now and next week-end I've got to decide about that.' She turned, pulled at his arm, and started across towards the goat-pen, almost dragging him.

Domingo was finished down there. He'd

poured the cat's dish full of thick, tinned milk again, and was happily watching her drink. The kittens were, as usual, falling into her, splashing the milk, rolling over and over locked in mock mortal combat.

Domingo didn't even hear anyone approaching until Fred and Jacqueline were close enough to see the kittens, and she emitted a little sound of delight. Then Domingo turned, smiled as his employer's granddaughter knelt beside the cage, and after that, Domingo raised his black gaze rather sardonically to Fred, asking some kind of question with his eyes which Fred chose to ignore.

Domingo had to tell her about the cat, how it had come dragging in, a forlorn, sickly, pregnant stray, perhaps seeking a quiet place to die, and how he'd brought it back to health.

Fred wasn't surprised at Jacqueline's delight; he had already seen how she loved other animals, horses for instance.

This time, he was left out while she and Domingo discussed the obvious strength, agility, handsomeness, of the individual kittens.

To Fred they were kittens; cute, in need of help and protection which he would certainly have provided if Domingo hadn't, but otherwise just cats.

Erin rang the dinner bell over at the house, which at least for the time being broke up Domingo's and Jacqueline's enthusiasm over the kittens. As they both arose, Domingo glanced sidewards at Fred, then suddenly remembered something back at the barn, excused himself with a hint of fatalistic resignation in his voice, and walked away.

Fred took Jacqueline's arm, turned and started back, once again, towards the house. She was less a woman now and more a girl. 'Did you see that rather dark kitten that sat back by himself? I think he should be named Fred.'

He looked at her without comment. He happened to know that little dark, thoughtful kitten was a female.

When they reached the grove again he kept right on walking. She lost some of her enthusiasm just before they emerged on the far side, and when she finally pulled him back to a halt she said, 'Fred . . . ?' and lifted her face.

This kiss was different. There was a quick flash of fire to it, from both of them, and afterwards she clung very close to him in total silence.

He could feel her heart beating at double-time, could feel the supple length of her pressing close, and was very conscious of something else that she probably hadn't even thought about: Her *need* for a strong man, more than her desire for one.

Then he saw her grandfather come out upon the rear loggia gazing down towards the stable, and eased her away very gently, turned and started forward again, saying, as he did so, 'I've got a guilty feeling about this. As though I were betraying your grandfather's trust in me, Jacqueline.'

She had that unique intuitive wisdom only women possessed, and proved it now. 'I think he would consider what's happening between us as anything but betrayal.' Then she felt for his hand, squeezed it, let go and said, 'It's not him I'm worrying about, anyway.'

'Esparza?'

'Not him either.'

'Your father, then?'

'No, Fred — it's me.'

Chapter Fourteen

AN END TO SECRECY

Erin Clancy, in her best conspiratorial manner, tapped the envelope beside Fred's plate at dinner, and in a lowered voice announced that Mister Spencer himself had put it there.

She and Domingo, perhaps waiting for Fred to open the envelope, kept watching. He folded it, stuffed it into a pocket and started eating his dinner. When Erin glowered, then marched back over to her stove, Domingo shook his head.

'Tomorrow night we get onion pie.' He did not elaborate and Fred did not probe, but what Domingo meant was that when anyone irritated Erin Clancy, she could be depended upon to retaliate by serving something she was sure no one could stomach.

Evidently in the opinion of Domingo Salazar there was nothing less palatable than onion pie.

After dinner Domingo and Fred strolled back outside, where a noticeable weightiness was in the night. Domingo immediately raised an appraising gaze to the heavens.

'No stars,' he announced. 'There is another storm building up.'

Fred paused to stoke and light his pipe.

Domingo, catching sight of movement in the direction of the study, where an amber light glowed, suddenly said in a lowered voice, 'I think three will soon be a crowd. I'll see you later,' and moved off the loggia striding down towards the patch of trees dividing house-area from the stable-area.

Domingo may have thought it was Jacqueline but it was her grandfather. He paced casually on over to where Fred was lighting up, hands behind his back, then stopped beside the larger and younger man, gazed around, saw the shadowy shape of the stableman going down through the trees, glanced at the sky and said almost the same thing Domingo had said.

'Another thundershower coming.'

'Good for the grounds,' said Fred. 'Particularly good for the roses.'

The old man nodded and dug round in his jacket for a pipe. Without even waiting to be asked, Fred handed over his pouch. Merritt Spencer laughed. It was the first time Fred had ever heard him do it. Spencer held up a striped pouch from another pocket.

'I owe you enough,' he said, and paused, still smiling, to catch the younger man's eye. 'You know, I wanted my son to take you back the day he brought you out here. That would have been one of the worst mistakes of my life, Fred.'

'Probably not, Mister Spencer, because I'll tell you something about me: wherever I go, there is usually some kind of difficulty. Not trouble; that is not *violent* trouble, although I've bumped into my share of that too. But difficulty.'

'Like Esparza and my granddaughter?'

'Something like that, yes. Or worse.'

The old man filled his pipe and lit it, put up the striped pouch and looked for a chair. There were none at this end of the loggia so he remained standing.

'Maybe it's not trouble hunting *you*, Fred, maybe it's you hunting *trouble*. Take my granddaughter for instance; I doubt if she ran to you.'

'You're right, she didn't. I butted in.'

'You see, then?'

'Mister Spencer, all due respect, sir — neither you nor your son, and certainly not Jacqueline, understand the rules of life the way men like Nick Esparza live it.'

Merritt didn't dispute that. He may have had some mental reservations, but there wouldn't be much point in dragging them out now. Not after Fred had usurped the initiative. Merritt puffed and simply said, 'Well, admittedly there *have* been a great many changes lately; in the past ten or so years. But I still don't approve of violence.'

'Neither do I, Mister Spencer. My idea of the good life would be,' Fred paused, removed his pipe and gestured with it, 'something like this: land enough to ensure privacy, handsome grounds, a good home, serenity. The hell of it is, everyone seems to be struggling to achieve something pretty much like it too, and there is just so much money and so much land to go around.' He plugged the pipe back between his teeth. 'And there's one other thing you non-violent people never seem to get through your heads. *I* don't want violence. *You* don't want violence. But the other guy thinks that's the only way he can achieve his ends, and usually, he's right, so don't convince *me* violence is bad. I'm already convinced of that. Convince *him*.'

Merritt shifted his weight. He did not enjoy standing for any length of time. He turned and pointed towards some chairs northwards along the porch, up near the French doors leading from his study. 'Come along,' he said, and led the way.

Fred hesitated. Not that he didn't enjoy his employer's company. He did. But he was full of Erin Clancy's good food and had intended to just sit out front of his quarters in the warm, hushed night, and think a little.

But he obeyed.

As they reached the chair Merritt asked if he'd like a dram of brandy. He declined, they sat, got comfortable, then the old man dropped a clanger. 'Odd thing about women, you know; they look different when special moods are upon them. As you know by now, I'm an observant man. Now I'd say that when Jackie returned from her ride this evening you two didn't fight. Although I'd bet a fortune that when she arrived here this afternoon she was ready to scalp you. So — my estimate of the situation is, my boy, that she's perfectly agreeable to swapping Esparza for you.'

Fred was thankful for the darkness. He heightened his camouflage by puffing up a cloud of smoke, and that also kept him from having to make a comment. Merritt didn't even look at him.

'She is a good girl. I've come to that conclusion lately, although I'll admit I had my doubts up until a couple of weeks ago. About the time you arrived, in fact. Not that there could be any connection, of course.'

Fred squinted for a closer look at the older man, but Merritt, if he was being sly, didn't show it in his expression.

'That's what I've been sitting in the study thinking about this afternoon, Fred. That's why I'm going to take a back seat. But mind you, I still deplore violence.'

Finally, Fred spoke. 'I don't anticipate violence, Mister Spencer.'

'Say; I wonder if you'd mind calling me just plain Merritt.'

'Yes sir, I'd mind.'

Fred did not explain and Spencer did not ask him to. 'All right. As you wish.'

'As I was saying, Mister Spencer, I don't anticipate violence.'

'I've got Esparza sized up differently than you have, my boy.'

'Maybe. There is one thing: someone is going to have to reimburse him for those notes your granddaughter signed. Money, he might fight hard for. But if I've read him right he won't put up any more of a struggle to keep Jacqueline than will be necessary to salve his pride. He's got lots of pride; his kind always has. But he's not in love with anybody but Nick Esparza. If he gets the money back, and if he realizes someone he doesn't even know might cause him to be hospitalized for a while, I'm gambling he'll be sensible. Of course no one must know about this, otherwise his pride will be injured.'

'I see. Fred, I hope you're right. How much money will it take?'

'I have no idea, sir.'

From behind them, over near the French doors, which had been open to admit the coolness, framed by amber lamp-light, Jacqueline said, 'Thirty thousand dollars — plus interest.'

The men whirled. She glided out towards them dressed in a long, pale blue frock that complemented everything about her, from her height to her golden colouring.

'Grandfather; I'm sick about it — so ashamed I could —'

'Hear, hear,' growled the older man, arising to offer his chair, which Fred was also doing. 'Never apologize in front of people not in the family. It's very bad form.' She didn't take his chair because Fred had brought over a separate one and had placed it between the other two chairs. She sat, thanked Fred, and clasped both hands in her lap.

'I just don't know why I let it happen, Grandfather. It was so — ridiculous — so childish and stupid. Fred is right; he says I'm stupid and he's perfectly right.'

Old Spencer raised his brows at Fred, and the younger man made a little shrug.

'But I wanted so much to succeed; to make you and Daddy proud of me because I'd proven I was a Spencer — someone with talent and —'

'That's enough,' exclaimed the old man, squirming and clenching the pipe between his teeth, palpably uncomfortable. 'Child, I've been proud of you ever since the first time I didn't have to boost you into the saddle. Talent? Land sakes alive, Jacqueline, you've got more talent than the rest of us ever had.'

'Grandfather, that's not true.'

'All right; I'll leave it to Fred,' stated the old man.

Fred's pipe had gone out. He stepped to the edge of the loggia to knock it empty, and turned back wearing a little crooked smile. 'I suppose we'd have to define talent.'

Both Jacqueline and her grandfather looked up at him. He didn't return to his chair at once, but stood there wearing that little crooked smile. 'If you mean acting talent — well — I'm certainly not qualified to judge except for what appeals to me, and I'd agree with you there, Jacqueline. But if talent means an ability to make people smile, or if it means an ability to make sunshine appear in a room where there was none until you entered it, why then I'd have to agree with your grandfather.'

Merritt sat a moment longer looking squarely

at the younger man. Then he said, 'I've got to say that was damned well expressed.' He arose. 'Fred, Jackie, it's been a long day.'

Jacqueline arose at once as though to speak but the old man held up a hand. 'Listen to me, sweetheart: The best way to handle trouble is to get it out in the open. All right; now we're no longer going to have to sneak about behind one another's backs, are we? So, that makes us allies, doesn't it? Then from now on that's how it is going to be.'

'But the money, Grandfather. I —'

'Never mind it was a lesson. An expensive one, but a lesson. Now excuse me, I've got to call Jay Logan, and if I wait much longer he'll be in bed and won't like being routed out. No — now that's the end of it for tonight, Jackie.'

The old man stepped around the chair and hastened across to the French doors, passed beyond and passed from sight.

She turned towards Fred with eyes made shiny by unshed tears. 'I feel sick,' she murmured.

He didn't touch her, didn't even go near her. 'I suppose you can make it up to him.'

'How? My allowance is ten thousand dollars a year from my mother's estate. It costs that much to live.'

'Well; perhaps he won't want the money, Jacqueline. He might be just as pleased if you'd forget prancing around on the stage in a few sequins.'

'Don't remind me,' she groaned, and sat back down again.

He finally stepped over near her, to his chair, and after sitting, leaned to take one of her hands and hold it. 'I know, if I were in his boots and you were my granddaughter, I'd want —'

'I couldn't be your granddaughter. Or even your daughter.' She turned, pale and very beautiful in the lowering night. 'I'm not sure what I could be to you.'

'I am,' he murmured, and leaned.

She didn't hesitate, but bent far forward to meet his lips. When he raised a hand to caress her hair she moved slightly under the pressure of his lips, and for a second that flash of deep-down fire in both of them nearly upset everything. Then she pulled away.

'I don't want to fall in love,' she whispered.

That puzzled him. 'Why?'

'Well; I don't know, exactly.'

'Esparza?'

'I suppose so. I haven't thought it through. It's probably because he uses the term a lot — falling in love — and he makes it sound — dirty. Like something that should be mocked.'

Fred leaned back and raised his eyes to the little square of light barely visible through the yonder trees, down at the stable where Domingo was probably blissfully sitting, bottle of beer in hand, watching television.

Life for Domingo Salazar was manageable, and that made it possible for him to face it head-on. For someone like Jacqueline it *wasn't* manageable.

Somewhere along the line it had mastered *her*, she hadn't mastered *it*. The result was anguish, doubt, fear, and a little dread of life.

But Fred said nothing about any of this. He simply kept holding her hand and sitting there, until she finally, very gradually, relaxed in the chair at his side.

Then he said, 'Everyone thinks there's another thunderstorm coming. What do you think?'

She looked, not at the sky, but at him. Then she arose, went over, sat in his lap and putting her face against his shoulder, began to softly sob.

He stroked her back and kept silent. He was good for her and they both knew it, but she also realized that she must appear in Fred's eyes as something less than admirable. At least that was what bowed her spirit as she sat there clinging to him, and meanwhile, overhead, the dark, thick sky got more and more grainy, more and more weighty and ominous, and eventually even a little soughing breeze began to blow, which was the harbinger of the downpour shortly to begin.

Chapter Fifteen

AFTER THE DOWNPOUR

There was no question about it, the best sleeping-nights were the wet ones. Fred didn't stir after he got to bed, excepting one time when the first raindrops fell. He listened for a moment to the increasing intensity, then rolled over and went back to sleep.

The downpour continued most of the night. It stopped some time after three in the morning. By six, although everything glistened and the air was fresh and clear, the sun was having a struggle trying to burn through the retreating, ragged host of soiled grey clouds.

Domingo's light was on, which meant he was up too, but he hadn't emerged yet so Fred went down to the goat-house and opened the door so the kittens could rush out into the wet grass, which they did, then halted in dismay as that chilly dampness greeted them. Their eyes were open now, so they peered all around, wrinkling their noses, and until their mother came forth to also sniff and look, they did not go very far.

Otherwise, the grass shone where cobwebs held transparent pearls, and when the sun finally burned through each of those tiny drops of water shone with rainbow colours.

Domingo finally emerged shrugging into a cotton jacket, looking at the sky, at the ground on all sides, and finally down where Fred was leaning, watching the cats. He started off in that direction.

'What can you do on a day like this?' he asked, by way of greeting. Domingo was pleased about the rain. 'No damned irrigating for a week. Now maybe I can get caught up around the barn.'

Fred cocked a sceptical eye at Salazar. 'Or snooze in the tack-room,' he said, and if Domingo would have accompanied his expression of reproach with some comment, he didn't get the chance. Erin Clancy rang the breakfast bell.

They went over to eat, and Erin Clancy smiled at Domingo, glanced at Fred with her smile stiffening a bit, then fed them. She evidently hadn't yet forgotten that Fred had not mentioned that mysterious envelope.

As before when a thundershower had arrived, the day was cool, and although it doubtless would have turned hot by midday as it usually did when the sun burned downward, they were spared that discomfort by some huge, white clouds, a veritable Invincible Armada of them, sailing majestically down from the north, to partially shield earth so that the heat was diverted all day long.

It was amply warm, even then, but when Fred

went out to remove a torn limb from one of the fast-growing Chinese Elms, it was cool enough to be pleasant, which aided him at his work.

He had the limb sawed off, had the bucket of black healing compound to the raw wound, and was critically examining his tree-surgery when someone coming across the damp grass without a sound, said, 'Very professional.'

He turned. Jacqueline was smiling in a teasing mood. He grinned back. 'Without an anaesthetic, too.'

She laughed, came closer, and as she examined the job he'd done he stood there admiring her. She wore a light blue sweater, a pair of well-fitting light tan jodhpur riding trousers, and had her ash-blonde hair held in place by a broad band, the same shade as the sweater. She looked tanned and healthy and wholesome.

'Beautiful,' he said.

She nodded without looking away from the tree. 'Yes, isn't it. Particularly the way you've applied that tar, or whatever it is.' Then she turned and he could see she was silently laughing at him.

Her mood was entirely different from last night. He could understand that, for aside from the fact that last night had been unpleasant and she wouldn't want to dwell upon it, this was the kind of a morning that would make people glad to be alive.

He asked if she was going riding, and instead of answering she cocked her head at him in a coquettish way and said, 'Any more trees to practise your skill on? I could carry the tar bucket and hand you the instruments.'

He said, 'None. If you'd like I'll saddle a horse for you.'

'No thanks. I've never seen you saddle a horse, but I've seen you *un*saddle one.'

He smiled wryly. It was true; he understood the fundamentals of saddling but did not appreciate any of the finer points of it.

'Fred; I telephoned my father this morning. He'll be out tomorrow to spend the week-end here. He wasn't wild about it, but I said it was important, so he agreed to come along.'

That was about as he'd expected it would turn out. But if her father hadn't come at all it wouldn't have troubled him very much. He didn't speak, so they stood gazing at one another a moment before she spoke again.

'Nick telephoned out here just after breakfast. He wants to see me in the city.'

'What did you tell him?'

'That it'd have to wait until Monday because I was staying out here until then.'

'He accepted that?'

Her expression clouded over just for a second, then cleared. 'Yes. But not very gallantly. You see, when he's told me to meet him somewhere before, I've always gone. He was a little annoyed.'

'Any idea what he wanted to see you about?'

'The Broadway play, he said. The man who

was revising the script finished it. He wants to go over it with me. But . . .'

'Yes.'

'It's probably just my imagination, but when he's wanted to discuss the play other times, he's usually also said we were a little short of money.'

Fred slowly nodded. 'Great chap, Esparza,' he murmured. Then he smiled at her. 'Come along. I'll let *you* saddle the horses and we'll both go riding.'

'Are you disgusted with me, Fred?'

'Do you want an honest answer?'

She hesitated, bit her lip, then nodded at him.

'Not disgusted. I know some things I didn't know before about you. But Esparza leaves a bad taste in my mouth. Now let's go get those horses.'

She fell in at his side, walked towards the stable with her head down, and said nothing. Obviously she was disgusted with herself. Perhaps, more than disgust, she was feeling chagrin.

As they stepped up on to the tanbark he cheered her up. 'Listen, love. I'm a healthy male animal, and riding across open country on a beautiful day with a lovely woman is going to make me say things you might want to strike me for saying.'

She flashed him a look, then preceded him on through the archway into the stable courtyard before saying, 'I've already told you — I don't want to fall in love.'

He stopped. 'With a roughneck gardener?'

She turned. They were secluded there in the little arched alcove. She stepped back, raised her arms to his shoulders, melted against him, and when his grip on her waist tightened, she sought his lips. When she could free herself she smiled.

'I *still* don't want to fall in love.'

'How do we manage and keep on doing this?'

'I don't know. You'll just have to help me.'

He started after her saying drily, 'You've got to be kidding!'

There were four horses in the stalls. He selected the same docile beast he'd ridden before, and let her supervise his saddling efforts. Domingo was nowhere in sight, not that either of them looked for him, nor even thought of him.

When they were ready, she showed him the proper way to mount — without putting his hand upon the cantle. He had no difficulty. She was graceful, physically supple and muscular. His private observation, as he watched her straddle her horse was that although she might not be able to act, and was only a passable dancer, she was, in her own environment and at something she liked and thoroughly understood, very competent.

They walked their horses southward out of the stable, did not look back hence neglected to see Domingo watching from over the lower half of a tack-room door, and when the sun sprang from behind a cloud to catch them with no shade anywhere around, it made them and the world they were riding through golden and delightful without also making it hot.

They walked halfway to the oak grove where she'd tried to strike him, then she eased her horse over into a right-lead gallop, and grinned as he booted his animal to keep up.

It was no race; she was a lifelong horsewoman; when she wished to get somewhere fast she used a car. The gait was easy to keep cadence with and Fred enjoyed himself. He grinned back.

They bypassed that oak grove and headed across a sunlighted low roll of grassy land towards a small stone hut he hadn't seen before, but then he hadn't explored the entire estate yet.

They approached, finally, at a walk, and she said, 'There is a man buried here.'

He was surprised, studied the little hut, which was old and mossy, the stones none-too-expertly cemented with crumbling mortar, the roof-slates faded from their original pale grey, and saw no headstone, no indication the hut was anything other than perhaps just the remnant of someone's ancient shelter when all this country had been unsettled and largely unexplored.

She showed him where to tie the horse then took him closer. Then he saw the little bronze plaque. It had been set flush in the ground. Unless a person was directly over it looking down it was hidden by wildflowers, grass and weeds.

He read it aloud, 'François Du Pré, *voyageur*, trapper, killed on this site by Indians, 1767.'

'My grandfather had the plaque made and put here,' she explained. 'That's all that's known about Mister Du Pré. There aren't even any legends. The old stone hut was his camp, and local legend preserved by the historical society told us the rest.'

Fred turned and looked out over the countryside. 'It's a good place for a camp,' he said. 'You can see anyone coming from any direction.' Then he smiled at her. 'But François must have been a heavy sleeper.'

She was watching him. Had watched him make that careful study of the countryside. Now she said, 'Fred; tell me about yourself.'

He kept smiling over at her. 'You've got most of it already from your father.'

'No. Not most of it. Only the bare outline. I want to know it all. What kind of a little boy you were, where you lived and what you did?'

He laughed at her, turned and looked for a dry place to sit. There was a bit of protruding shalestone nearby so he went over to that with her following along. When they were seated he said, 'I was born in Massachusetts. My father was an army officer. Both he and my mother were killed in an aircraft crash when I was twenty. But I was already in the army, so, I just kept at it. Nothing very spectacular about that.'

'Israel . . . ?'

He shrugged. 'The odds seemed a little uneven. I went along with six other guys.'

'Those men who visited Nick . . . ?'

'Three of them, yes. They were commandos. We all were. Well; when things quietened down we went down to Germany and hired out driving trucks through blockades on the autobahn. Nothing very spectacular about that either, except that we were paid about ten times what we were worth.'

'There was danger,' she said, trying to draw him out more.

He smiled at her. 'There is danger in crossing a busy street. No, actually there was very little danger. Oh, Ivan used to glare and scowl and call us names in Russian, which we didn't understand. But Ivan's orders did not include shooting at people at that time. Then that died down and we split up. Three of the other lads were from the U.S. so we flew home, pockets full, and split up again. The other lads stayed in Europe.'

He raised his arms in a gesture of finality, and dropped them. 'That's about the size of it. Now then, what about you.'

She looked away from him and very slowly looked back again. 'Would you like me to start with now and work back?'

He nodded.

She blushed. 'I'm in love,' she said very quietly. 'That takes care of right now.'

He took her in his arms and the sun slid behind another of those great clouds, covering the earth with a mantle of warm shadow.

Chapter Sixteen

'I LOVE YOU!'

It was past noon when they left the old stone hut and rode around the estate, following a barbed-wire fence most of the way, until, within sight of the mansion, barbed-wire gave way to the white-painted post-and-rider fencing, and there she showed him her grandfather's skeet range.

There were four little huts, three-sided affairs that all faced southward. Out front sixty to eighty feet was a cement pad with a steel plate set in it where the skeet-shooter was installed when anyone was there shooting clay pigeons.

She said her father didn't like to skeet shoot; shotguns bruised his shoulder and he wasn't a very good shot anyway.

He asked if she liked it and she nodded. She'd been target shooting since she was large enough to fire a shotgun without being bowled over by the recoil. He thought of a small blonde girl in dead earnestness tracking a clay pigeon, then screwing up her face when she fired because she knew what was going to happen when the gun went off.

'What's amusing?' she demanded, halting her horse to gaze over at him.

'You. For a dozen reasons. But at this spot, how you must have felt just before firing.'

She laughed. 'I had to do it. My grandfather should have had a grandson. He didn't, so I had to make that up to him.'

'You understood that when you were a child?'

'Yes. Little girls may grow up to be stupid *big* girls, but when they are still little they're a lot smarter than little boys about some things.'

He was willing to accept that. 'Does your grandfather still have a couple of shotguns?'

She frowned at him. 'Yes. A whole rack of them. But he doesn't come up here any more — and you're not going to get me up here either. I'm past the age where bruised shoulders are a badge of toughness.'

The clouds were overhead, scarcely moving, but they were thunderheads, not rain clouds. They kept down the heat though, which was welcome, and from time to time they also hid the sun. On the ride back towards the stable great cloud-shadows sailed across the countryside, dark and definite and soundless. It was like watching the collision of two worlds, one tangible, one intangible.

Fred was thinking something like that when Jacqueline said, 'How will it end?'

He looked at her. 'Don't worry about it.'

'No,' she retorted, 'I didn't mean — about Nick. I meant about us.'

He kept looking at her. 'How would you like it to end?'

She swung back forward in the saddle and gravely studied the stables, still some little distance onward. 'I don't know, Fred . . . I'm afraid.'

'No need,' he told her. 'It will be up to you, Jacqueline.'

'You said you loved me.'

'I do. I meant every breath of it.'

She still rode facing stonily forward. 'And I stopped fighting it back there at the stone hut.' She turned. 'But suppose it doesn't work out? After the other thing I've been through, I don't think I could stand another body-blow.'

He had no way to reassure her except with calm words. He said, 'Look, Jacqueline, there are no guarantees about anything in this life. But there is something just as good. Honest effort. If we really want it to work, then it will. I don't know what else to say — to reassure you.'

'I don't know why I'm so afraid of it, Fred.'

He had a hunch. Her father's personality was such that very probably, although he had remained married, as a child Jacqueline must have seen something, perhaps coldness or indifference, on the part of her parents. He didn't ask any questions about that, though. He let her ride along at his side for a fair distance, then leaned, touched her hand, drew back and when she turned he smiled.

'Honest effort?'

She nodded and at once her eyes misted, then she leaned to be kissed. It was one thing not designed specifically to be accomplished on horseback, but it could be done.

As she drew back she said, 'I'll make an honest effort.'

After that they were quiet all the way back to the stable, and in fact even their horses were silent enough so that when they finally left the turf and crossed into the courtyard, Domingo, who was cleaning stalls up at the far end, didn't hear them at once. Then, when he raised up and turned, he smiled, put aside his implements and went forward to help with the horses.

'A nice day for a ride,' he said, standing back until Jacqueline had dismounted. She nodded at him, handed over the reins, then went around where Fred was standing and waited. He took her by the arm and started off. Domingo peeked after them, shrugged, waggled his head, and went back to look after the horses.

As the sun sprang out again, but only temporarily because another cloud was gliding towards it, Fred and Jacqueline left the archway and crossed to the yonder grass on their way towards the manor. She walked so close that occasionally they brushed hips and shoulders.

'I'm hungry,' she said, as though nothing else was on her mind.

He looked down disapprovingly. 'How can you think of food when you've agreed to marry me?'

She faltered in stride, then quickly recovered. 'Did I? I don't remember being asked.'

She smiled and he slid an arm round her waist as they approached the fringe of trees separating house and barn area. 'All right, I'll marry you. But . . .' she didn't finish it, she only looked a little uneasy, then forced another smile as he halted in the first shade and looked down. 'Nothing. Nothing at all. Forget I said it.'

He kissed her gently, started to draw away but she reached and held him close, and this time the kiss had fire in it. He blew a ragged breath afterwards, shook his head in a reproving fashion, then smiled.

'Remember what I said about being a male animal. Another kiss like that and I'll —'

'Never mind! I can guess.' She reached for both his hands, stepped back and looked long at him. 'It's crazy, Fred. I'm not even out of my last predicament and here I am already involved in another one.'

'There will be a difference, and also, this will be your last one.'

She said, 'Yes,' very tenderly. 'Fred? Why didn't you arrive last year? Or even early this spring?'

He laughed. 'I came as swiftly as I could.'

She returned the little laugh, dropped his hands and glanced once up towards the manorhouse. 'Should I explain this to Grandfather?'

'If you wish. But your grandfather's a pretty keen-eyed gentleman. I don't think you're going to shock him.'

She widened her eyes at him. 'Oh?'

'Well; he made some innuendos last night when he and I were alone on the patio.'

She shrugged. 'All right. I'll tell him anyway.

But I won't know all of it.'

'All of it?'

'You asked me to marry you, didn't you?'

He grinned. 'Excuse me. I didn't understand.' He kept gazing at her. Finally he said, 'Wasn't there something about the fifteenth of next month . . . ?'

She squeezed his hands, dropped them and turned to walk on up to the house. Over her shoulder she said, 'You and Grandfather ought to get on very well, both of you being so practical. He won't want all that planning to have to be cancelled, either.'

Fred laughed. She turned, for the last time, at the end of the spit of trees, waved, then passed from his sight.

On the stroll back to the barn he recalled most of what they had said to one another. He hadn't asked her any personal questions although he'd answered all her questions. He knew enough to realize that what was most important to him was how he felt towards her.

He hardly knew her father at all, and what he did know didn't make him eager to strengthen their acquaintanceship. But her grandfather was altogether different. There was already a bond between Merritt Spencer and Fred Nufall.

In most ways they were different, but basically their principles and convictions were similar. They were both men with strong wills, direct approaches, and a kind of hard-headed practicality.

'Hey!'

Fred came out of his reverie only a few feet from the overhang out front of the hired-help's quarters. Domingo held up an opened bottle of chilled beer with a wide grin.

Fred hadn't even felt thirsty until that moment. Now he did.

As Domingo handed over the bottle and stooped to pick up a second bottle, already sampled, he shot a narrowed look at Fred. 'I told you. Now look at the fix you are in.'

Fred grinned, took two big swallows from the bottle and stepped around Domingo to a chair. 'I'm in a fix all right. I missed lunch.'

Domingo snorted. 'You are going to have someone mad at you. She is already engaged.'

Fred looked up. 'Domingo, you are a nosy devil. Did you know that?'

'Who has a better right? I taught her to ride a horse. I used to take her to her Campfire Girls meetings, and when her father told me he didn't want her riding horses so much because she might get hurt, and also because it was for tomboys, not nice little girls, who was it who argued with him until old Mister Spencer came down and sided with me so she could at least have that much fun out of a pretty bad life for a little girl? I, that's who. Each time it was I, Domingo Salazar.'

Fred raised a hand. 'All right, Domingo, all right. You win. You're not nosy, you're just exerting a special interest. Well; it's no secret: I'm in love with her.'

Domingo drained his glass, dropped into a

chair and said, 'Good,' with resounding candour. 'Fine. Now all you have to do is not get your throat slit when that gangster finds out. Hah!'

Fred smiled. 'Any suggestions?'

'One. Run.'

They both laughed, then Domingo turned serious. 'It's a good idea. You could go away with her. Stay away for a year or two. Any man, even that gangster, will be over his mad by then.'

'I've never been a very good runner,' said Fred dryly, and sipped more of the beer. It was cold and tangy and very pleasant. 'And Esparza wouldn't forget. Not on your life, he wouldn't.'

'So then?'

Fred finished the beer, studied the label on the bottle and spoke very quietly. 'So then, my friend, the gangster and I have a little talk, and whichever one of us blinks first, loses.'

Domingo stared. '*Caramba!* You haven't read in the newspapers about Nick Esparza?'

'Yeah, I've read about him.'

'If you aren't afraid then you must be thick in the head.'

Fred laughed. 'I'm that too. Come from a long line of thick-headed sauerkraut-eaters.' He shot up to his feet. 'I need a shower.'

'No. You need a priest,' exclaimed Domingo, and also arose. 'I'll go down and feed the cats, then if you need me I'll be somewhere around the stables.'

'Need you for what?'

'Well, I don't know. But you are certainly going to need *someone* when that gangster comes out here breathing fire.' Domingo thought a moment. 'On second thought, maybe if you need me I won't be around.' He grinned and sauntered off down the tanbark walkway in the direction of the goat-house, and Fred, watching him go, laughed softly to himself.

The clouds were breaking up, finally, as the day advanced. Some of them were being shredded by a howling high wind that neither moved a leaf nor made a sound down upon the earth, although it did make those cloud-shadows flee more swiftly over the hills and meadows.

As long as that wind blew it would not be possible for more thunderstorm-clouds to accumulate overhead and perhaps dump down more water, which was a blessing. The rains were welcome, but not so close together. It would be much better if they arrived at ten-day intervals.

Finally too, with the last thunderheads torn and battered off towards the distant horizons, the sun had the whole heavens to itself, so the heat immediately increased. But it was too late in the day for very much discomfort to ensue.

Chapter Seventeen

AN ARGUMENT

The first Fred knew that events might be accelerating was when he stepped outside of his quarters after showering and changing, and saw Harold Spencer striding briskly across the turf towards him.

He had only infrequently considered Merritt Spencer's son, and always as someone only indirectly concerned with either Merritt or Jacqueline.

Also, he had expected Harold to arrive the following day, not this afternoon — or evening, since it was getting along towards dinner time again.

He had seen enough men stride in anger to guess that Harold Spencer must know at least part of what had been transpiring at the estate. He thought he could also surmise Harold Spencer's feelings towards himself.

He felt the irate man's feelings were justified, but primarily because he didn't think Harold Spencer really understood what was going on. As he leaned upon the cross-piece out front of his quarters now, waiting for Spencer to see him, to let fly his hurled denunciations, he also thought that of all the people likely to be in the wrong, Harold Spencer was probably foremost.

But of course that was something Fred might think, but could not mention. For some reason, it was usually considered very bad form to tell a man his offspring's difficulties were the result of his own failures as a parent.

Spencer finally saw Fred, and his onward thrust slackened slightly, but not very much. When he came on up he said, 'Nufall, the day I drove you out here after the interview, as I recall you said your interest was simply working out-of-doors, with your hands.'

'That's what I said, Mister Spencer.'

'But it seems you've developed some other interest.'

'Meaning, Mister Spencer?'

'My daughter!'

Fred studied the man's florid face with its expression of hostility, then said, 'It's pretty complicated to just stand here and explain, Mister Spencer. But there was nothing devious about it, if that's what's in the back of your mind.'

'What is in the back of my mind, Nufall, is that none of my family needs another complication. But particularly my daughter.'

Fred agreed. 'You're perfectly right.'

Spencer had screwed up his courage for this encounter, and evidently he hadn't considered the likelihood of assent. He relaxed slightly, some of the high colour left his face, and the hostility in his glare diminished somewhat.

'Then what were you thinking of, to let my daughter fall in love with you?'

So that was it; Jacqueline or Merritt Spencer had told him this. Evidently they *hadn't* mentioned the Esparza affair.

'Mister Spencer. I don't know that anyone ever *lets* someone fall in love with them, any more than I can explain why I fell in love with your daughter. But —'

'Just a minute, Nufall,' broke in Harold Spencer, his tone softening to a steely hardness. 'It couldn't possibly be that my daughter will be a very rich woman when her grandfather dies, and after that, when I die.'

Fred continued to lean and stare at the other man. When his rising resentment was well under control he said, 'Would it suit you if I signed a legal Agreement never to touch a dime of her money — or yours or your father's money?'

Harold snorted. 'It wouldn't be enforceable. Once my father dies and she inherits her share from him, she would probably hand it over to you.'

'Look, Mister Spencer, I don't want the money.'

'Of course not. No one ever wants money.'

Fred waited again for the rising annoyance to dissipate. 'Mister Spencer, I can't match you dollar for dollar, but I can take care of Jacqueline fairly well. I'm not destitute.'

Harold Spencer thought about this. 'Soldiering doesn't pay that well,' he ultimately muttered.

'I haven't always been a soldier, Mister Spencer. At least not an orthodox soldier.' Fred straightened up off the cross-piece. 'But whatever I've been, I think it's likely to compare with what Nick Esparza has been.'

Spencer shot his answer right back. 'Do you realize Nick Esparza is a very bad person to cross? If you think, just because my daughter swears she is in love with you, is going to make Nick offer you clear access, you're in for a very rough, and probably painful, disillusioning. Now, then, Nufall, if you want to take that risk, that is quite up to you. But I'll not see my daughter endangered.'

Fred had to repress a feeling, and a look, of disgust. 'Knowing what Esparza is, I don't understand how you could let her even associate with the man, let alone marry him.'

'She told me she wanted to marry him.'

Fred started to retort, then slowly closed his lips. There was no way to make Harold Spencer into something he was not. Pointing out what an irresponsible father he had been would only put something between them neither would ever forget.

He sighed, finally, and said, 'Well, Mister Spencer, if you have something specific in mind I'll listen to it.'

'Leave,' was the answer that came right back, with the velocity of a bullet. 'Gather up your things, and I'll personally drive you back to Chicago tonight.'

'What will that solve?'

'For one thing, thinking of your own skin, it will get you away from here before Nick arrives. For another, Jacqueline will forget this ridiculous summertime interlude with the yardman, and come back to her senses.' Spencer put a hand in a coat pocket, and Fred stopped him.

'Don't make it worse,' he warned. 'If you had in mind using your cheque book, forget it. As for leaving: If your daughter wants that, I'll leave this evening, without the inconvenience of having you drive me back to the city.'

'My daughter? You know perfectly well she won't want you to leave.'

Fred left the overhang area, strolled around in front of the cross-piece he had leaned upon, and said, 'In that case, Mister Spencer, why don't you just let us work it out? She's of age. So am I.' He forced a little smile. 'A lot of people make mistakes. Maybe she and I are making one, as you believe, but it won't be the first mistake for either of us, so, speaking for myself, I'm going to be very careful.'

'And what, may I ask, do you propose doing about Nick Esparza?'

'So far I haven't met the man. But being aware of his probable resentment, I'll think of something.'

Harold Spencer threw up both hands. 'You'll *think* of something! Mister Nufall, I'm disappointed in you. I had some idiotic notion you'd be wise and realistic and tough.'

'Sorry to disappoint you.'

'And there is something else; you've got my father believing in you too. Now you certainly realize that he is in his late sixties, has led a sheltered life for the past few years, and is hardly able to cope with this kind of a mess.'

'But you are,' said Fred, and shook his head. 'Mister Spencer, it's been your discussion all along. Right up to this point. Now I'm going to tell *you* something: Butt out! Your daughter and I want your goodwill. I'm sorry you got so upset about us caring for one another. But it's our business, not yours. There are a lot of Nick Esparzas in this world. Maybe you've only known this one. Maybe you have an ability for closing your eyes to things you don't know how to handle. Well, Mister Spencer, that's your hang-up. Mine happens to be Jacqueline's happiness. Esparza doesn't give a damn about that.'

'You don't know what you're saying; he's in love with her!'

Fred gently shook his head from side to side. 'The only thing in this world he loves is Nick Esparza. He would use her to open a lot of doors for him. That's all. And I'll tell you something else, Mister Spencer; when he had all those doors open he wouldn't need your daughter any more.'

Spencer's colour returned. 'You realize, don't you, that what you've just said makes me look as though I were derelict as her father?'

Fred did not answer that. 'Listen; what I want

is a life as different from Esparza's strata as I can make it. That's what I want for Jacqueline too. I'm trying to explain something to you, Mister Spencer: Your daughter means an awful lot to me. I want to see her laugh a lot, and not have to paint her eyes nor prance around on a cheap stage. I want a natural, pleasant, good life for her.'

The dinner bell interrupted. From a short distance away Domingo Salazar emerged a little apologetically from his quarters, threw a darting, self-conscious stare at the adversaries — he had naturally been listening to every word — then fled off towards the main house. Neither Fred nor Harold Spencer more than glanced at him.

Spencer then said, 'If you really want to help my daughter, Nufall, get out of her life.'

Fred smiled. 'That sounded like something out of a B-movie. People don't get out of other people's lives any more, Mister Spencer, just to avoid unpleasantness.'

'I'll tell you something, Nufall: You are going to get yourself killed.'

Fred kept meeting the other man's irate look through a short interval of silence. 'They are probably waiting dinner for you, Mister Spencer.' He straightened up, glanced past, then hesitated as though wishing Harold Spencer to move out first.

Spencer did not move.

They studied one another. Fred thought that what he saw in Merritt's son was the beginnings of resignation. Hostility towards Fred, but resignation towards what Fred was doing.

There was no question of Harold Spencer's strength of character; he had very little, if any. He had never needed any, which was fortunate. Fred knew his type to be brave enough, even intelligent enough, but just never quite strong enough because they had grown to manhood without ever actually requiring much strength. Everything was always done for them — for a fee, of course, but then they'd always had the fee — or their fathers had had it.

He even pitied Harold Spencer slightly, so he eventually said, 'It'll work out. If you think Esparza is likely to think you somehow caused Jacqueline to drop him, I'll make sure he finds out differently.'

'You are, my friend, a very great fool. He will not think I influenced her alone. And he also happens, according to the newspapers, to have any number of underworld connexions. What can you do?'

'Just try, Mister Spencer. Just try.'

Spencer rolled up his eyes. 'Great gawd, Nufall, you simply cannot be this naïve. Moreover, you have no right to get Jackie involved in Nick's vengeance. Or all the rest of us, for the matter of that.'

Fred said nothing. He let Spencer have his say, then he started on past without speaking. They had said it all, anyway, and although that last remark of Spencer's had some validity — everyone in the family was now involved — that had never been Fred's wish nor his intention.

Of course that changed nothing. The others were definitely involved. As he strolled towards the house he speculated a little on that.

Esparza would, of course, believe that Jacqueline had betrayed him. He was even justified in feeling that way, ego aside. But it was probable that his backlash as far as Merritt or Harold Spencer were concerned would not amount to much. He probably viewed Harold with contempt; most men who had clawed their way to the top, even illegally, would view Harold that way.

As for Merritt, Esparza was unlikely to think there could be much satisfaction derived from having the old man mugged.

By the time Fred reached the back door of Erin Clancy's special domain, Harold Spencer, cutting diagonally across the grounds, was approaching the loggia in the direction of his father's study where the French doors stood ajar. He did not turn and glance northward or he'd have seen Fred thoughtfully eyeing him.

It was, by this time, well along towards late evening, but daylight was still predominant, and the night shortly to arrive promised to be another of those quiet, soft, warm and velvety ones.

He entered the house, passed through the rear porch, the pantry, and entered Erin Clancy's brightly lighted kitchen to see both Erin's eyes, and Domingo Salazar's eyes raised in frank and lively inquiry.

He smiled, said not a word, and went to take his place at the table.

Chapter Eighteen

A MOONLIGHT WALK

It was a beautiful night. The stars were larger than life, the moon was approaching its seasonal fulness, and the recent rains had unlocked all the powerful natural fragrances.

When Jacqueline came down from the house Fred smiled in the shadows out front of his quarters, knocked out his pipe and turned to his companion. Domingo said, 'Well; tonight there are no cowboys. I only watch the cowboy shows. So now I have to go watch that other junk.' He arose. They hadn't got around to discussing what Domingo had overheard of the argument between Fred and Harold Spencer. Fred had offered no openings and Domingo had felt uncertain about creating any. So now he simply arose and went walking away.

Fred smiled at his retreating back. He had understood exactly what Salazar's earlier mood had been, and what it was now. Fred did not feel resentment about Domingo eavesdropping. He was fond of Salazar, but more than that, Domingo'd had every right to be in his quarters when Fred and Harold Spencer had had their conversation. Even if Fred had wished to admonish Domingo, it wouldn't have been justified.

As Fred arose and stepped ahead to lean and watch Jacqueline approach, he promised himself that someday, if he got the chance, he would explain things to Domingo. Very often it was easier to explain difficulties to people who lived a life of difficulty than it was to explain things to people whose wealth and intelligence protected them from trouble.

He called softly while she was still a hundred feet away. 'Hello; are you a moonbeam or a goddess?'

She smiled, pleased, and covered the last few yards like that. Then she said, 'Father is furious. He came stamping in, late for dinner, and demanded that Grandfather get you off the estate, and that I call Nick up and make peace with him.'

'And?' he asked.

'Grandfather looked as black as thunder. He said no one, least of all his own son, could burst in upon him at mealtime shouting, and that if Father didn't mind his manners Grandfather would order *him* off the estate.' Jacqueline smiled. 'It would have been interesting if it hadn't also been serious. Father sat down and ranted on, but he kept his voice lowered. And Grandfather ate his dinner as though my father weren't even at the same table. In the end, though, he told father to either face up to his responsibilities or go back to Chicago, that he didn't care which.'

Fred smiled. He had only seen brief flashes of old Merritt's wrath, but he knew that it lurked not very far below the surface; the right set of circumstances would bring it out.

He started to offer Jacqueline a chair, but the light in Domingo's window, plus the discreetly ajar door changed his mind. He took her by the hand and started slowly walking down towards the inky archway passage, and from there out into the moonlit stable courtyard where the scent of hay and leather and horses was very pleasant.

He told her of the talk out front of his quarters with her father. She walked along, holding his fingers, listening but seemingly not concentrating on the subject. Finally, when she'd allowed him to say it all, she looked up.

'Grandfather thinks us being married here on the fifteenth of next month is wonderful.'

He stopped. 'You weren't listening to what I said.'

'Yes, I was listening. Do you want me to repeat it? It was simply that it didn't seem as important as the other thing.'

She smiled in the moonlight, tilting her face to him. He hung back but only for a moment, and in the end his private conclusion was that he'd been telling everyone not to worry, that he'd take care of things, and now it seemed that perhaps one of them, at least, was taking him at his word.

But right after that kiss she dropped a clanger.

'Nick telephoned right after dinner. He'll be driving out in the morning.'

Fred still held her, but the desire of a moment earlier slowly dissolved as he thought of this fresh development. He had told Harold Spencer he would think of something. Well; now was the time. Or at least sometime between now and morning.

Right at that particular moment it was hard. Jacqueline's hair smelled of some faint, aromatic soap. It was as soft as silk when he lowered his face to rest a cheek against her head.

They resumed their stroll, passed through the southern opening leading across the rolling, soft turf, and that oak-grove where she'd just explained about Esparza, seemed a lot farther on foot than it had on horseback.

But they veered off to avoid that onward shade, because now in the moonlight, the bright places were more desirable. What was daytime shade in the oak-grove, at night-time was dark gloom.

He said, 'What is it you want of life, Jacqueline?'

She leaned to brush close when she answered. 'Peace, I suppose more than anything else. Peace, and sunshine.' She looked up quickly. 'Not necessarily comfort and leisure, but a place to laugh and — well — maybe to raise a family.' She hesitated, watching him, then said: 'A horse? Maybe a dog?'

He laughed. She wasn't answering him, she

was trying to say the things she thought he wanted her to say. 'Anything else?'

'You.'

'I can provide those things. Not the way you'd have them here at the estate, but somewhere. On less land, probably, and certainly with a lot smaller house.'

'I'll help, Fred.'

'That's exactly the point, love. Your father has an idea that's part of my reason for wanting to marry you.'

She didn't explode with indignation. 'I got that feeling from listening to him at the dinner table tonight. He didn't actually come right out and say it, but I got the impression it was behind his words.'

They were west of the oak-grove. Another few hundred yards and they would be approaching the little stone hut. He veered off again.

'I have some money,' he told her. 'Not a whole lot, but more than enough, I think for a nice small place somewhere.'

She took his arm and held it close. 'I don't care. If you simply wanted to put up a tent it would suit me fine.'

He grinned down at her. 'And when the thunderstorms came?'

She smiled back. 'Well, of course I meant a *waterproof* tent.'

They passed around beyond the oak-grove, startled a nocturnal skunk who reared up on its little legs to sniff and probe for them with weak eyes. When they saw him, the skunk had located them and was swapping ends with his handsome tail aloft and gently vibrating.

They stood back and waited. They were still well out of range and obviously meant the little animal no harm, so after a bit he lowered his flag, squared around to make certain they were coming no closer, then he lowered his black nose and continued to sniff the ground, evidently on the spoor of a fieldmouse or some similar small and burrowing animal.

Jacqueline said, 'My grandfather and I once went into the chicken business together. The hens were mine and I had to take care of them, and he would buy all the eggs for the house. I think it is quite possible that a forefather of that skunk was what put us out of the chicken business. Did you know skunks love chicken — raw, I mean?'

He grinned. He hadn't known it; didn't in fact know anything about skunks except that they were to be avoided. 'Your grandfather was a great guy, wasn't he?'

'Yes. And he still is.'

'It hurt him when you didn't come see him.'

She nodded, clinging to his arm. 'I know. But you see, I wanted so hard, just once, to do something without anyone's help.'

He made certain the skunk was not going to take offence if they moved, and started on again without saying any more about her neglect of Merritt Spencer.

Her reason for not driving out to the estate was valid enough, if the way she chose to seek success was not. But she knew this now without any chiding from him about it.

They skirted the far side of the grove and long shadows thrust southward as far as their feet, made thin and weak by the distance and by the moonlight. A night-hunting owl skimmed in low, saw them at the last possible moment because it had been concentrating on the grass where nocturnal rodents fed, and with a great flop of astonishment flipped over almost on to its back beating both wings madly, which was the first sound it had made. Owls were silent hunters even on the wing.

Jacqueline instinctively pressed close to Fred, startled almost as badly as the owl had been. When the bird was frantically beating its way upwards and away, he slid an arm round her waist.

Then they laughed together. She said she wasn't really very brave, which really didn't have very much to do with being startled, but he told her she was as brave as she'd ever need to be, and she kissed him in the moonlight, clung to him for a while, and said she felt at peace for the first time since she'd been a little girl.

He heard the beat of her heart, quicker now than it usually beat, and felt the pressure of her body when she breathed. It was a wonderful moment for him.

He said, 'You know; this is something I've often wondered about. How would it happen when it finally happened to me. And maybe it won't sound very sensible, but when I decided to get a job in the country — to sort of let my hair down for a while working with my hands around plants and maybe animals, but anyway in a different environment than I've been used to, I actually had a feeling this is how it might happen.'

She snuggled close, snickered and said, 'That's a terrible sentence.'

He pushed her back and she laughed up into his face. 'Well; in school we were taught never to mix infinitives, nor drag the sentences out.'

'How would you like to be bent over my knee and paddled?' he asked, then they both laughed as she broke free and darted back out of reach.

'Here I am baring my heart to you — baring my soul in fact. And you're studying sentence structures!'

'You win,' she said a little breathlessly. 'I'll never do it again.'

She moved back inside his arms, stood on tiptoe and sought his lips. This time, when his arms folded inward, he squeezed some of the breath out of her and she made a little gasping sound. Then he released her, found her hand to hold, and said, 'Anyway, terrible sentence-structure or not, you are the loveliest thing that has ever happened to me. I had no idea I could be so deeply in love.'

She sighed and they moved on, staying just beyond the brush of oak-shadows, until, bending back around towards the north-east, they could see tiny orange pinpricks ahead where the manor-house stood. It looked like a light-and-shadow painting propped up in the midst of a greyer world of land and distance.

'Honest effort,' she mused aloud, saying his words from their former time together. 'My grandfather said that was wonderful. He said you had a flair for the right words.' She squeezed his fingers. 'He also said you were a handsome, compelling personality.'

He was a little embarrassed. 'Nice of him. But I'd have liked it better if you had said it.'

'But I did. I said you were beautiful.'

He stopped. 'Beautiful! How can a man be beautiful? Women can. You can. In fact, you *are* beautiful. But not a man.'

She laughed. 'You'd be surprised how many times women say that about men. And some are. You, for instance. You are wide-shouldered and narrow hipped, and your face is — well — a little like a pirate's face, but still beautiful.'

'That,' he told her, 'will be enough of that.'

They kept walking. Somewhere a very long distance off a dog barked. There were other estates roundabout, as well as a number of farms, most of them quite old in terms of residency.

They saw another owl, too, but this one saw them first and tipped upwards slightly to go sailing overhead without making a sound.

Then they were close enough to make the house out more clearly and she said with a little sound of resignation, 'Why can't nights like this go on forever?'

'For one reason; because even we beautiful men need our sleep.'

She looked up at him. 'You really are, even if you don't believe it.'

Chapter Nineteen

THE LONG WAIT

He was working on the south side of the main house the following morning when he saw Jacqueline drive out, swing to her right on the county road and go scooting off in the direction of the village.

He assumed she was going to do some marketing for Erin Clancy. He did not believe she would be gone long if Esparza was shortly to arrive.

In fact that was why he'd chosen his particular location this morning: it offered an excellent vantage point to watch the roadway. He would be able to see Esparza's car long before it reached the front gate.

It also happened to be cool over among the tall shrubs, trees and flowers where he worked, which was a blessing, because at long last the heat was returning and there were no high clouds to blot out the sun.

He hadn't been out there very long before Merritt appeared, dressed in his baggy old tweed coat and wrinkled gaberdine trousers, pretty much the way he'd been dressed that time they'd had their first serious talk over in this same general area.

Spencer seemed cheerful, for some reason. He said, 'Well, I'll certainly say one thing for you, Fred: You liven things up.'

They exchanged a smile, and in a nearby tree an oriole scolded them unmercifully for being in his private area.

Fred said, 'I'm sorry about the argument with your son yesterday.'

'Pshaw,' grumped the older man. 'You weren't as hard on him as I was later, at dinner. Anyway, Harold has no stomach for something like this. He never has had, I'm sorry to say.' Merritt turned, squinted up the empty roadway and mused aloud. 'Maybe Esparza won't show up.'

Fred said nothing. Esparza would show up. A challenge to a man of his nature couldn't go unanswered. At least that was how Fred was privately betting.

Merritt turned back and spoke as though Esparza was no longer important. 'Have any close friends you'd like to invite for the fifteenth of next month?'

Fred thought a moment. 'Three, perhaps. No more that could get here.' He straightened up and looked directly at Spencer. 'There's something I suppose I ought to tell you. I'm sure it's come up, and will probably come up again. Jacqueline's money.'

'Not around me it won't come up again,' exclaimed Merritt. He made a hard smile at Fred. 'I'll tell you something about women with money that possibly hadn't occurred to you: If a strong man with honour marries them for it, they're nine times out of ten one hell of a lot better off than if they'd married some socialite with the backbone of a jellyfish, whether he married them for it or not. Money is important, don't misunderstand me. You can't make money any more unless you have money. But it's not the curse to romance people seem to think.'

Fred thought that over, then grinned at Merritt; the older man had a pragmatic wisdom that was different from any other hard-headedness Fred had ever encountered. It would be easy to learn things from him.

'Speaking of money,' Spencer went on, 'I've had a packet of it sent out from the city. It's locked in my desk. Fifty thousand dollars. That ought to take care of Mister Esparza, eh?'

'I thought thirty thousand was enough.'

Merritt shrugged. 'If thirty thousand is enough, think how much nicer fifty thousand would seem to him. I understand your opinion is that he'd sell his soul for cash. Well; I figure to try and act as the devil's emissary.'

A car approached from the north. Both men turned to stare. But it cruised right on past and Merritt made a grunt. It was one of his neighbours, he informed Fred.

That scolding oriole finally decided that since the two-legged things weren't going to leave he would, and with a flash of splendid colour swooped out of his tree and went winging off to a more distant tree. Merritt saw him, watched a moment, and eventually said, 'I bought a dossier on you, Fred,' and at the younger man's quick look, Merritt shrugged. 'Well; I'm being candid about it, so later on you won't think I'm just a nosy old man. The fact is, I needed the reassurance after I saw how things were going between you and my granddaughter. Anyway . . . it's very interesting. As a young man I used to dream of doing most of the things you have done. Only I got bogged down in finance and business, and when I could get loose, I was too old.' He smiled. 'Some time maybe we could sit and talk. I'm an incurable romanticist. I love to hear tales of derring-do.'

Fred nodded, still keeping quiet. Now and then he flicked a glance northward up the road. It wasn't really necessary to look; if a car had been coming he'd have heard it before seeing it, in the rural stillness.

'If I'd ordered a husband built to specifications for Jacqueline I couldn't have done any better,' went on Merritt. 'What she needs, thrives on, you've got. Strength and understanding — and affection. By now you've figured out the kind of parent my son was. Well; no more need be said on that score.'

Merritt dug into a coat pocket and Fred almost smiled as he reached for his pouch and held it forth. Merritt accepted it without comment, proceeded to fill the pipe he'd been digging for, and afterwards passed back the pouch with a nod of thanks. 'Pretty strong,' he said, with a twinkle in his eye. 'I guess one or the other of us is going to have to change brands, eh?'

They laughed, but the sound of another approaching car, this one from the south, caught and held their attention. It was Jacqueline returning from her trip to the village. She came rushing up the drive and didn't see them. They didn't move, and there were the shadows, so she whisked on past, drove around the north side of the house bound for the kitchen area to unload the car, and as Fred started to drop his eyes back to Merritt Spencer, another movement returned his attention to the long, marble loggia along the front of the mansion.

It was Harold, and if his daughter had overlooked the two men standing in shade some yards distant, Harold saw them and started in their direction.

Fred had a misgiving. He knew how Merritt felt and he also knew how Harold felt. He didn't want them to fight in front of him.

'I guess I'd better go put up my tools,' he said. 'Be noon shortly.'

Merritt, still unaware his son was approaching across the grass from the rear, said, 'If I knew what you had in mind, Fred, I'd know how to act. The money, for instance. Should I brace him as soon as he arrives, take him to the study and hand it over — or what?'

Harold was still a hundred yards away. Fred said, 'I thought he'd be paid by cheque, Mister

Spencer. That we could hold off on that end of things until I'd had a little discussion with him.'

'I see. That's why you were working out here this morning?'

'Yes. I would like to nail him as he gets out of his car and before he enters the house.'

'Anything special in mind?'

'No sir. Just a little talk; put some facts on the line. After that send him back to the house.'

'And that is when I'm to intercede about the notes — about buying them?'

Fred nodded without speaking because Harold was only a couple of yards away. Finally, his father heard, and turned. They exchanged a look, neither smiling, and old Merritt continuing to puff on his pipe.

Harold looked past at Fred. The stare wasn't as hostile as it had been the day before, but neither was it friendly. 'Anything I should know being discussed here?' he asked, and Fred, resenting the way Harold was bypassing his own father, as though Fred, not the old man, were master here, said, 'That'd be for your father to say, Mister Spencer.'

'Not by a bit,' snapped Harold.

Fred's patience snapped. He didn't dislike Harold Spencer. He hadn't analysed his feelings but if he had he might have found that he felt a little sorry for Harold Spencer; felt a little gentle contempt as well. Now, he said, 'Look, friend, yesterday I bent backwards so you and I wouldn't have anything to recall in years to come that would be some kind of barrier between us, for Jacqueline's sake. Now take my advice, Mister Spencer, and do the same thing. Because if you don't — I've had about all your lip I'm going to take.'

Harold wavered between accepting the advice and denouncing it. His father puffed and regarded him closely, and eventually reached out a hand to take hold of his son's upper arm in what could have been a little shake of affection.

'Come down off your high horse, Harold. This isn't a fight among us. It's us against Esparza, with Jackie's happiness at stake.'

Harold still didn't drop his eyes nor speak. Merritt removed his hand and tamped ash in his pipe-bowl. He'd had his say.

Fred kept waiting. He knew something Harold probably didn't know: When a man is going to attack, has made up his mind to do it, he doesn't stand staring, because the longer he does that the less resolve he has.

Fred smiled. 'Esparza will soon be out of our lives, one way or another, Mister Spencer, but I have a feeling you and I will know each other for a long time after we've forgot him. At least that's how I'm protecting my thoughts and actions.'

He slowly thrust out his right hand towards Harold. It was a critical moment for all of them. It was also that kind of a moment for Jacqueline, she was inside the house, probably in the kitchen with Erin Clancy, and was blissfully unaware.

Fred kept that hand out but his smile was beginning to congeal a little round the edges.

Then Harold Spencer took the hand, pumped it, and said, 'All right. But I certainly hope you know what you are doing.'

'What *we* are doing,' said his father, faded eyes beaming quiet approval.

Harold nodded. 'I stand corrected. And of course you're right, Nufall. It's Jackie's happiness that matters. And we'll have to stand together, too.' He faintly scowled. 'But it's not something I like being involved in.'

Neither Merritt nor Fred made a comment about that, although doubtless both of them could have, because no one actually *liked* being involved in unpleasantness, but sometimes it simply couldn't be avoided.

The oriole returned, found three instead of two of those two-legged things down there and went into a shrill paroxysm of indignation. The men ignored it.

Someone came out of the house. They all heard the door close and looked over in that direction. It was Jacqueline, and she didn't see them until they started to move off, which they did when Fred picked up his tools, saying he thought he'd better get back to work.

Harold and his father, for the first time, went strolling back towards the front of the house side-by-side, heads lowered and quietly talking.

Fred looked over their heads, saw Jacqueline looking the same way, down where he stood, and felt the tug of her presence even over that wide a distance. Something very personal sang over the interval to him, from her. He smiled and she smiled back. Her father and grandfather could just as easily not have been within a hundred miles.

Then they were closer and she dropped her eyes as her father said something. Fred continued to watch the three of them.

He had hoped never to have to challenge Harold, but it had come, and now he was pleased the way it had turned out. He thought Merritt was also pleased.

Finally, he turned and started off in the direction of the tool-shed, and the moment he stepped out of the shade that midday sun struck him like a blow.

He squinted skyward but there were no more promises of rain; not a cloud was visible and the sky was a faded, brassy blue. Mid-to-late-summer was on the land. There would be no relief now until autumn when the winds came howling down across Lake Michigan out of Canada.

At the tool-shed he encountered a mud-dauber wasp busily at work constructing one of those mud nests under the eaves, where it would eventually seal in an unconscious spider or worm with one wasp-egg.

He gave the mud-dauber a wide berth. They had a very unpleasant sting, and this was the one time of year a person could be expected to be stung without actually very much provocation.

Over at the stable Domingo came ambling through the archway bound for his quarters. Soon now, Erin Clancy would summons everyone to lunch.

Fred closed the shed door, looked at his watch and frowned. If Esparza had said he would be here this *morning,* he would have to arrive within the next half hour to keep his word.

Chapter Twenty

THE PAY-OFF

Fred stoked his pipe and returned to the far side of the mansion, this time entering the arbour with the stone benches where he and Merritt Spencer had first talked. He looked at his wrist, looked at the road, and for the first time wondered if perhaps Esparza might not arrive.

If not, then Fred would have to go to the city and seek him out. Whatever came out of his relationship with the others, this particular matter had to be settled first.

He picked up the sound of a car approaching from the north, held the pipe down from his face and waited for the first sighting. He didn't know Esparza's car, but that didn't trouble him; he would know when it came because men like Nick Esparza never drove ordinary cars.

It came. He knew it was the correct one the moment sunlight menacingly glistened off the sleek, black bonnet.

Fred stopped, knocked the pipe empty, pocketed it and arose to stand with one foot on a stone bench, arms bent across the knee, relaxed, expressionless, and unblinking.

The car slowed, made a flashing turn, out in

bright sunlight, then started slowly on up from the yonder roadway. It was time for Fred to move.

He left the arbour, timing his arrival over in front of the house to coincide with the car's halting over there.

Once, as the car passed close, Nick Esparza's head turned. He was wearing oversized sunglasses. They stared shiningly and darkly out at Fred, then passed onward with no expression showing, and the car slowed to a near halt. Fred hastened his steps to cross over and reach the side of the car before Esparza alighted. One tanned, large hand shot out, grasped the door from the outside and opened it.

Nick Esparza glanced up, then, evidently thinking this was an act of courtesy, this holding the car door open for him to alight, twisted and stepped out of the car.

Fred's other hand reached, almost slowly, casually, caught hold of Esparza's arm and pulled him gently away.

The dark man looked astonished. Fred closed the door, dropped his hand from Esparza's arm and said, 'Do you see that little rose-arbour yonder with the stone benches in it? Well, Mister Esparza, turn now and walk over there.'

The dark man was still astonished, but he flushed, finally, and pulled his mouth. 'What the hell are you talking about; who are you, anyway; what do you think you're doing?'

Fred answered none of it. 'Turn, Mister

Esparza. Turn and walk over into that nice shade over there.'

The dark man's anger finally overcame the astonishment. 'You go to hell,' he snarled, and whirled as though to march up the steps to the loggia.

Fred's right hand was a blur of motion. The edge of his hand caught Esparza in the rib-cage and the swarthy man gave a quick, sucking gasp. Fred's left hand reached and very easily turned Esparza, who was in pain and beginning to bend forward slightly.

'To the arbour,' murmured Fred, steering the dark man by the arm.

They were passing from hot sunshine to blessed shade before Esparza overcame the pain that slice in the ribs had caused. He started to turn, to speak, but Fred gave him a rough little shove the last ten feet into the arbour, and Esparza was too busy keeping his balance to say anything for another moment.

The shade was pleasant. Hot, but pleasant. Fred turned Esparza towards him, swiftly patted his body, then pushed him down upon one of the stone benches, and finally Esparza's eyes widened in some kind of understanding that this thick-shouldered, bronzed man across from him wasn't just someone's yardman after all. Those patting hands, knowing exactly where to feel for a concealed weapon, had told Esparza what he now knew.

He puckered up his brow. 'Say; who the hell

are you, anyway?'

'Just listen for a moment,' Fred retorted, stepping back to the other bench and leaning upon it while he regarded Esparza carefully. 'Do you by any chance happen to have those notes with you?'

Esparza reached up, removed his eye-glasses to disclose close-set, black, feral eyes that seemed locked in a perpetual squint. He blinked in an intent study of Fred. 'What notes are you talking about?' he asked, speaking quite slowly. 'Listen, buddy, if the Spencers think they can hire some punk to —'

'The Spencers didn't hire me, Esparza. And you know which notes. The ones Jacqueline Spencer signed, and that you bought. *Those* notes.'

Esparza had finished his scrutiny of Fred and would have replaced the glasses but Fred leaned and knocked them from his hand. Then he smiled at the dark man.

'Mister Esparza, when I ask someone a question I like an answer — fast!'

'Yes! I have those damned notes with me. What of it?'

Fred kept on smiling. 'Just happen to be carrying them?'

'No! I never carry them.'

'Then why today?'

'It's none of your damned business. And let me tell you something, punk —'

'Esparza! You've got me mixed up with some

hoodlum. When *I* say punk that's what *I* mean. A hoodlum, a hotshot-mugger, a gangster. A punk in my language means you.' Fred paused, still smiling. 'Now let's start over again. And Esparza, one warning: Answer cute one more time and I'll break every rib you've got, then your neck.'

Esparza whined. 'What is this? Who hired you? If it wasn't the Spencers how come you're after those notes?'

Fred lied. 'You're entitled to that much explanation and no more. I want those notes because some men in a syndicate who could buy and sell you out of a vest pocket want Harold Spencer. The notes will be how they'll get him. Now that's enough. Tell me why you happened to have the notes with you today?'

'Okay. The girl's been troublesome lately. I was going to give her one last chance to shape up — then toss 'em down in front of her father and grandfather to let them see what kind of a sweet young thing they've got.'

Fred stared thoughtfully. It sounded reasonable. He decided on a long chance and said, 'How much are they worth, Esparza?'

At once the black, feral eyes brightened. 'Thirty-two grand, including interest. Why; do you want to buy them?'

Fred held out a hand. 'Let me see them?'

Esparza's attitude changed. He fished out a white envelope, handed it over, then lit a cigarette while he watched Fred sift through the documents in the envelope. He even smiled.

'Listen — whoever-you-are — you pay face value plus interest and you're welcome.'

Fred closed the envelope and pocketed it. 'Welcome to what, Esparza? What about the Broadway play?'

'There isn't one. The girl didn't play ball so there isn't one.'

'And the marriage?'

That time Esparza's eyes flickered. 'What about it? Look, do you want to pay full price or don't you?'

'Esparza, I asked about the marriage!'

'Okay. Okay. If you buy those notes at face value there won't be a marriage.'

'Why not?'

'Are you blind, man? Because the minute your syndicate moves against her old man she'll know where they got the leverage — from me.'

Fred had to move fast and make changes. In a stall he said, 'How do you want your money; cash?'

Esparza stared. 'You've got it here?'

Fred smiled. 'Here and in cash. And a pair of lead boots if you ever open your mouth concerning this, or if you ever go near the girl or the other Spencers again. Or — if you try to finger me.'

Esparza took a big drag off his cigarette, his face suddenly changing expression. 'Mister,' he said softly, 'do you know anything about some guys who burst into my apartment and —'

'Mugged you, along with three of your friends?'

'Yeah.'

Fred smiled broadly. 'I wouldn't know a thing about that, Mister Esparza. Now you stay right here. Don't walk out of this arbour if I'm gone an hour. If you do, take my word for it, you'll go home tonight wrapped in a black blanket. Do you understand?'

Esparza nodded, inhaled, exhaled, and slowly turned his head to make a long, deliberate examination of the grounds, the trees and their shadows, the distances on all sides.

Fred stepped out the back of the arbour, strode off towards the stable area and did not change course until he was beyond Esparza's sight. Then he swung back and ran to the loggia out back of Merritt Spencer's study, forced the French doors open, and found himself under the candid stare of Harold and his father.

He ignored the younger man, stepped to the desk and held out a hand. 'Thirty-two thousand dollars.'

The older man didn't even hesitate until he'd lifted a fat envelope to drop it upon Fred's palm, then he looked up with a perplexed scowl. 'It's the full fifty thousand.'

Fred tore the envelope open, counted the money, divided it into two piles and tossed one back upon the desk. 'Stay in here,' he said, 'and make certain Jacqueline also stays inside.'

Harold was nervous. 'How is it going? You realize that he probably is armed, don't you?'

Fred did not reply. He didn't even look at Harold as he pocketed the money, stepped back out through the French doors and retraced his steps until he was back in the stable area. Then he jogged southerly until, hidden by trees and shadows, he was able to stalk back half the distance to the arbour. He halted to make a long, careful examination of the arbour and the man sitting there lighting another cigarette.

Esparza seemed impatient but otherwise at ease. When he killed the light he leaned back to inhale, then stare over at the mansion with a cold, speculative expression.

Fred stepped from the shadows and sauntered on back. Esparza saw him, finally, straightened on the bench and got a look of quick, cold interest on his face. To Fred, it looked as though Esparza's greed was at its height. He had been counting on that, but he hadn't really expected Esparza to sell out this easily. Evidently money meant more to the swarthy man than even Fred had guessed it might.

Entering the arbour, Fred said, 'It's all right. There isn't going to be any trouble after all.'

Esparza blinked. 'Trouble?'

'There are some big names in the syndicate. Very rich businessmen. They don't like the idea of letting you walk away knowing what they are up to.' Fred smiled that same cold, menacing smile again. 'Those three who paid you the visit — there are now eleven more. Someone suggested taking care of you and those three who were with you when you got your shellacking. I told them for thirty-two thousand you'd probably keep quiet.'

'That's a promise,' said Esparza, showing no fear, but showing greed again. 'You got it?'

Fred brought forth the money and counted thirty-two one-thousand-dollar notes into the dark man's outstretched hand. When he finished he reached, peeled off one note and slowly pocketed it.

'Do you mind?' he asked softly.

Esparza's eyes narrowed, but only momentarily. 'No, it's all right. Maybe I owe you that. Maybe you're lying from top to bottom too, mister.'

Fred leaned on the bench again, slowly nodding. 'Maybe. If you think that — maybe another visit from those other three might help you remember that the only thing you have to do is stay away from the Spencers, particularly the girl, and never open your mouth to a soul about what happened here today. Otherwise you're going to end up as dead as a mackerel, without knowing when the hit is coming or who is going to give it to you. It's just that simple.'

Esparza fingered the money, folded it carefully, pocketed it, then arose putting his sunglasses on again. 'I never welsh on a deal, mister.' He stood a moment regarding Fred with his old insolence and arrogance. 'Am I allowed any questions?'

'Just one: when you can shove off. The answer is — right now. Drive off and keep right on going. Esparza?'

'Yeah?'

'Don't kid yourself.'

They stared at one another a moment longer, then Esparza shrugged. 'Okay. If the Spencers somehow engineered all this — hell — all I wanted was a piece of their money anyway.'

'The Spencers don't know a thing. As for the money, don't try to find out who paid it and make noises like you want another shakedown. You're not playing in the same league at all — punk. Now shove off!'

Esparza turned, strolled to his car, climbed in and with little more than a casual glance towards the house, drove on around to where he met the main driveway, and kept on going. Fred watched him as far as the gate, then watched him wheel to the left and begin to pick up speed on his way back to the city.

Chapter Twenty-One

THE QUIET AFTERMATH

Fred continued to stand out there in the arbour a bit longer going over everything that had transpired, again, carefully and thoughtfully.

He finally straightened up, glanced towards the house, saw no movement, no faces at a window — which he probably wouldn't have seen anyway, the distance being what it was — then he started back around towards the french doors leading to the study.

He had no illusions about not being watched, but he wished to give the Spencers time enough to return to the study.

He smiled a little over this, but each time Nick Esparza came to mind again, the smile diminished.

There was something else; he'd resolved most of the details, but the unknown factor, of course, was Esparza's reaction now that the man was free and on his own. Time, of course, was the only answer to that.

As he stepped up on to the loggia and started for the doors he spied Domingo Salazar crossing from the tree area between house and stables towards the north end of the stable building where the hired-help's rooms were.

That made him pause a moment, but before he'd had much time to speculate on what Domingo had been up to, Harold Spencer appeared in the yonder doorway beckoning him.

Inside, old Merritt was lighting a pipe. He was seated behind his large and handsome mahogany desk and as Fred entered he looked up.

Fred tossed that one-thousand-dollar note on the desk, went to a chair and sat down. 'My cut,' he explained, 'for acting as intermediary. But I told him you people were not involved.'

Harold scowled. 'He won't believe that. He probably wouldn't have believed it even if you hadn't met him right here in my father's yard.'

Fred shrugged. 'That's up to him. He agreed not to approach any of you again. Particularly Jacqueline.' Fred tossed the envelope containing the notes in front of Merritt, who had ignored the bank note but who pounced upon the envelope.

'Of course he can't be trusted,' said Harold.

Fred gazed at the younger Spencer. 'When you size up a man, Mister Spencer, your only way of knowing how correct — or incorrect — you are, is by testing him. Putting him into positions where he will react the way you predicted, and if he does, why then you are more than possibly right about the other reactions he will evince. My guess about Esparza from the start has been that he is both very greedy and very egotistical. Well; the greed got assuaged a little while ago, and although the ego might have got a little bent out there in the yard, no one saw it happen, presumably, but the two of us. He knows I'm not going to say anything, and it's a certainty *he's* not going to. So he can afford to forget it. Of course the unknown factor is — will he forget it.'

Merritt, through shuffling through the notes, looked up. 'And you think that he will?'

Fred smiled slightly at the older man. 'I think so. There is something else he will undoubtedly consider: He was mugged a while back, and he'd never seen the muggers before. Which means that his underworld contacts came up with nothing about those muggers. That is going to influence him a lot. It's one thing to have enemies you know on sight, and something else to have enemies you don't know at all — that can walk up to you on any crowded street and hit you.'

Merritt puffed and looked satisfied, but his son said, 'About this mugging: Did you by any chance arrange it, Mister Nufall?'

Fred looked over at the younger man. 'Yes, Mister Spencer, and it can be arranged again. I told Esparza that it could, and added some untrue embellishments. If he believes my story, there is a syndicate out to ruin you.'

Harold's eyes shot wide open. 'Me?'

'Yes. The story was that was the reason someone was willing to buy your daughter's notes. So they could use them against you. Mister Spencer, in this kind of a situation you can't just leave a lot of loose ends lying around. That excites more curiosity than it lays suspicions. Esparza listened. Whether he believed me or not, or whether he'll still believe me a month from now when nothing happens to you, is his business. But he got his cash, and perhaps as time passes he will lose interest. I'll promise you one thing, though. If he doesn't lose interest he may get mugged again. That's up to him.'

Merritt was watching both the younger men with a tough twinkle in his eye. He removed the pipe and smiled at his son. 'I agree with Fred. He needed something particular.'

Harold didn't return his father's smile. 'Well, I suppose so. But I'm not delighted at being used quite like this.'

'No one is delighted about any of this,' replied the older man. 'But it all happened.'

'If you've judged this man incorrectly,' said Harold, 'we may all be in for more trouble than we'll like.'

Fred couldn't disagree. 'Right,' he said, and put a steady look upon Harold. 'And what were the alternatives?'

Harold subsided, as well he might, but his father, who had been living with all this a little longer and could afford to feel less bitter although all the expenses thus far had been borne by him, said, 'The point is, lads, that we'll simply have to wait and see. Esparza's been paid the money, I have the notes, which I'll destroy of course, and after that I imagine we might as well go right along living our normal lives until Esparza moves. If he does.' Merritt looked at them both, then went on speaking. 'I only know what I read in the newspapers, about hoodlums, but when Esparza first started coming round I made a study of him. Money and power impress him. Nothing else does. He fears them both. Now gentlemen, it would be very easy for him to look us up in any of the credit sources listing millionaires in the nation.'

'What's your point?' Harold asked.

'That if *he* wants to renew hostilities, using hoodlums, we can certainly afford to hire five-to-one with him.'

'He wouldn't believe we'd do that, father.'

Merritt saw the look of distaste on his son's face. Fred saw it too, and smiled. 'You wouldn't do it,' he told Harold, still smiling. 'And there wouldn't be any need for your father to do it.'

Harold squinted at Fred. 'But you would?'

Fred kept right on smiling. 'I would.'

'Would you know how?'

'Yes.'

Harold looked helplessly at his father, whose expression showed, that for a man who did not believe in violence, he was grinning toughly in support of Fred Nufall.

Harold fluttered his hands. 'All right. That's how it stands now. But I certainly hope it's finished.' He glanced at his wrist and pushed up out of the chair without much enthusiasm. 'I'm tired,' he said, 'I think I'll turn in.' He nodded towards his father, towards Fred, and went to the study door and closed it after himself.

Old Merritt watched his son depart with a wooden face, then went to work on his pipe getting it ready to smoke again. 'Anyway you look at this business,' he commented, 'Esparza's lost the initiative. Without the notes — no blackmail. Without the assurance we are his sitting ducks, he'll hesitate.'

Fred made a wry remark. '*With* thirty thousand in cash he's got all the salve for a bruised spirit anyone could ask for. But your son is apprehensive.'

Merritt's head whipped upwards. 'My son is always apprehensive. All his life he's been opposed to people who rock boats. When the rest of us have forgot Esparza, Harold will still be muttering to himself and looking over his shoulder.'

The old man reached, picked up that thousand-dollar note and dropped it upon the edge of the desk nearest Fred.

'It's not pay, just something I want to give you.'

'No thanks,' said Fred, and would have arisen but the old man spoke again, holding him in the chair with words.

'Listen to me; I want you to take that note and use it in some way that will please my granddaughter. We've grown apart these few years. I no longer have much of an idea of what pleases her in the way of presents. I want you to get her something.'

'From you, of course.'

Merritt puffed a moment. 'Well; why not just make it from you?'

'I said no thanks.' This time Fred arose.

Merritt shook his head at him. 'You're the most obstinate young man I've ever known. That's a thousand dollars.'

'I know what it is. Now let *me* tell *you* something. If you hired me to do what I did with Esparza it would have cost you as much as you gave him. And as for buying Jacqueline something — if I do that it will be with my own money.'

'I see. You have enough?'

'What does that dossier on me say?'

'Not very much about finances, I'm afraid.'

'Then you'll just have to take my word for it that I have enough.'

Merritt arose. 'Wait,' he said, and went rummaging over on a very old, hand-carved Spanish sideboard. 'Brandy?'

Fred watched the older man at work and made a tough little grin. He didn't want any brandy, but then there had been other times when it had been easier to bow to Merritt's will than to waste breath arguing. The fact of the matter was, he didn't like brandy.

Merritt held out a glass partially full, lifted one for himself and smiled at Fred. 'Welcome to the family, Fred. The Lord knows it's been a long wait.'

Merritt didn't elucidate and Fred did not ask

what that meant. He knew, or at least he thought he knew.

The brandy had a hot, biting feeling to it. Merritt said it was a new bottle, that it was a product of Germany. He seemed to be quite an authority on brandy. He even gave Fred a little thumbnail sketch of the legend behind the brandy.

Fred respectfully listened. But the story didn't make the stuff taste any better. Still, he finished it, stepped past to put aside the empty glass, then he faced Merritt and said, 'If you'll excuse me now.'

The old man nodded. 'Of course. One more thing, my boy.' His eyes twinkled but he did not smile. 'In case anything goes wrong, will you let me know well in advance of the fifteenth? There's quite a bit of work involved, you see, and having nearly had to postpone everything once, I wouldn't want to go through that again.'

'Nothing will go wrong, Mister Spencer. I love her. She seems fond of me.'

Merritt nodded. 'More than fond.'

'But there is one thing; I haven't asked her father yet.'

'Pshaw! Young people don't do that any more. They make up their minds, then as a rule they rush right out and track down a minister. Anyway, Harold has already been asked . . . hmmm . . . maybe I should have said Harold has been *told*.'

The old man swished his brandy and looked

down into the oversized glass. 'Good luck, son,' he said, looked up fleetingly, his faded eyes soft, then he turned abruptly and retreated behind his desk, his voice turning crisp, the way it most often was. 'Well; don't stand about in here. I think you'll find her down at the stable.'

Fred considered Merritt Spencer a moment longer, then wordlessly went to the doors giving out upon the loggia, passed through and stood in afternoon sunshine for a moment trying to see movement through the intervening trees down in the stable area.

It did not occur to him that he hadn't heard the noon bell that usually summoned the hired help to lunch. He had no thought farther from his awareness at this moment than food, anyway.

He wasn't sure Merritt had been correct about Jacqueline being down at the stables either. He hadn't seen her for some time and would have thought she might be upstairs in her room, after all that had happened this morning.

But a hunch told him the old man just might know something Fred *didn't* know. For a fact Jacqueline and her grandfather had been drawn closer together lately, thanks to their equal opposition to Nick Esparza and their equal approval of Fred Nufall.

He left the loggia and went striding down towards the nearby screen of trees where there was slanted wisps of shade, was halfway through in the direction of the stable when he caught sight of her down there in the coolness of the archway, watching him move towards her.

She was dressed for horseback riding and looked cool, long-legged and very lovely. He came forth from the trees at a slower pace because it gave him more time to study her. She was without any doubt, very beautiful, and now she also seemed very radiant.

Chapter Twenty-Two

A HAPPY ENDING

Jacqueline only made one reference to Nick Esparza. When Fred smiled at her, stepping on to the tanbark from the turf, she said, 'He's gone?'

'Half-an-hour ago,' he replied. 'With the money, and your grandfather has the notes. That ends it.'

'Does it?'

He nodded. 'I believe it does. But of course that's up to him.' Fred stepped closer, getting into the shade of the archway. 'If he decides to resume his interest, then I suppose I'll resume my interest in him.' He reached to touch the smooth coolness of her cheek. 'Don't fret about it. Whatever happens isn't likely to happen for a long while — if ever.' He leaned to seek her lips. They too were like cool velvet, and after he'd kissed her there was a very noticeable change in her. She smiled, felt for his hand, squeezed it and said, 'Domingo has the horses saddled,' and turned to lead him on through and out into the courtyard where he saw the horses. He also saw Domingo.

Salazar's dark, shiny face was blank. The black

eyes though, were full of a lively curiosity. Fred groaned inwardly; there would be more explaining to do. He was tired of even the subject of Nick Esparza. If he never heard the name again it would be just dandy with him.

Then he noticed the red-and-white checkered cloth tied to Jacqueline's saddle. She winked at him. 'A picnic,' she said. 'Unless everything got all soggy out here in the sun while I waited for you.'

Domingo grinned, finally, and stepped to the head of Jacqueline's horse to steady it while she mounted. It was an unnecessary act, but it gave Domingo an excuse for standing around, listening.

Fred's horse stood drowsily when he climbed across its back. Evidently this beast, the one he always rode, had made its own private appraisal, had found Fred thoroughly predictable, and therefore no longer had to keep a wary eye open.

Jacqueline led out. Fred let her get fifty feet along towards the open country beyond the stable before following. He used that distance to lean from the saddle as Domingo widely and knowingly grinned, and say, 'In case you thought you were very clever, I know you were hiding around the side of the house while I was talking to Esparza.'

Domingo's expression underwent a swift and complete change. From a broad smile it turned to a look of pained astonishment. 'What are you saying; that I was eavesdropping?'

'That depends on how close you were, my friend.'

Domingo thought, then said, 'I was close enough, but I only heard a very little.' He reached into a baggy pocket, drew forth something darkly shiny, and when his thumb made a pressure on the black handle, a six inch double-edged blade came out, shiny as newly minted silver.

'You see that hand-rag hanging on the post?'

Fred twisted in the saddle, saw the rag, and before he could nod, the rag quivered as six inches of highly polished, razor-like steel struck it, the tip of the blade burying itself in the post with a solid, meaty sound.

Domingo smiled upwards. 'You can never tell, amigo. Just because a man has no gun doesn't mean he can't be carrying something else.'

Fred reached to let a hand lie lightly upon Domingo's shoulder for a second, then raised his head as Jacqueline's fluting call came back. 'Thanks, partner,' he said, and moved the horse out.

Jacqueline was waiting. When he came up she didn't ask what he thought she might want to know — what he and Domingo had talked about — she eased her horse out at his side and said, 'Do you like cold chicken? Well; maybe by now it's *tepid* chicken.'

'I love it,' he assured her. 'My favourite plate is tepid chicken.'

Her eyes twinkled. 'And tepid beer too?'

'It's the only way to drink it.'

She laughed at him. 'That's fine, because I'm sure it's no longer cold.'

'The English drink warm beer.'

She made a face. 'I'm not fond of it cold or warm. It's terrible-tasting stuff.'

He was solemn now. 'There. There it is.'

She was baffled. 'There is what?'

'Our first argument.'

He wasn't smiling but by now she understood that he never smiled when he teased. 'And the world is standing still until it's resolved.' She smiled. 'No; our first argument was when I said you were beautiful. You didn't like it.'

'I liked it,' he corrected her. 'And of course you were perfectly correct. It was just that I had to be modest.'

She looked ahead where the oak-grove looked invitingly cool, led the way in among the trees, and at the same spot where she'd tried to strike him not very long before, she jumped down and went to tie her horse.

He took his cue from her. After all, this was her little party. By the time he'd tied his mount she was down on her knees spreading the red-and-white checkered cloth on the grass. He saw an ant, small, quick and inquiring, hoist itself at once upon the edge of the cloth. He told himself that now their picnic had assumed that one indispensable, for surely that confounded ant would race home, alert its entire community, then hasten back leading them.

He knelt to watch. She moved with sure, confident gestures and the way her jodhpurs were tight-drawn from waist to thigh when she leaned, and the way her cotton blouse stretched with solid fulness, made him want to touch her.

But he didn't. Instead he fished for his pipe, loaded it, lit up and sat in the blessed coolness gazing over the land in the direction of the stable. Then he moved slightly and saw the upper storey of the Spencer mansion above the trees. Finally, he looked back at her.

She held out an opened bottle of beer to him. Their hands touched, lingered briefly while they both held the bottle, then she blushed and turned to finish laying out the picnic.

'As lord and master,' she said, 'you're supposed to idly sip beer while I do all the work.'

'Of course,' he agreed, and when she looked around they smiled into one another's eyes.

Even when there was no bright sunlight to touch her, she looked golden. Her throat and face, her hands and wrists, were beautifully tanned.

He went to a little tree and sat with his back to it. He had seen enough of the world and the people in it to know that no matter where he searched, nor how long he looked, he would not find another woman like her.

He was also aware that she was just a little uncertain, perhaps even afraid, of what he might privately think of her for the foolish things she had done.

He drank beer and thought back over the past few years remembering foolish things *he* had done that were much worse, and he smiled indulgently over where she was putting the finishing touches on their picnic.

She finished, reared back on her haunches and beckoned. He moved over closer to her at once. She almost moved away when his arm slid towards her waist, but not quite. She turned, twisting to meet him, raised her arms and encircled his shoulders with them.

'I'm happy,' she whispered, making it sound soft and at peace. As though she were also drowsy.

He held her, let her rest her head against him, and was perfectly content not to move for a while. She burrowed closer, until he said, 'Food, madam is what makes men good-natured.'

She still clung, but slowly raising her face she said, 'Only food?'

'Brazen woman,' he said, pretending to scold. 'Do you realize we are being watched?'

She stiffened slightly and turned, gazing around. He reached down upon the cloth, picked up a frantic black ant and held it for her to see. 'Hundreds of eyes; they are everywhere.'

She looked at the ant, dropped her arms, turned and gave him a hard shove. He went back in the grass and she dropped across his upper body, kissing him, hard, then, when his arms came up she rolled clear and took a position beyond his reach, began to fill a plate with cold chicken, potato salad, sliced cucumbers and tomatoes, and when he sat up she shoved the plate at him.

'You wouldn't want me to do anything all those watching eyes would see — so eat, my love.'

He accepted the plate. 'Speaking of eyes,' he said. 'Did you know Domingo has been keeping tabs on us?'

She nodded briskly. 'Of course. What else is there for Domingo to do around here when he's not looking after the horses — or sleeping in the tack-room. Anyway, he's been like a father or an uncle to me ever since I was a little girl. If he's watching, it's to be protective.'

Fred chewed chicken and soberly nodded. He was remembering the way that six-inch steel blade flashed through the air without a sound, and struck the post.

'Someone else is also interested. My father. He didn't even explode when I told him I was going to marry you.'

'But he wasn't very delighted,' said Fred.

She puckered her brow a little. 'That's what I expected. But — well, you don't really know him very well — anyway, he just sat there in his chair gazing at me, and after a bit all he said was, "You'd better know what you're doing this time, Jackie," and then he offered his congratulations.'

Fred found the topic of her father out of place, so he held up a gnawed drumstick. 'This is delicious. Remind me to tell Erin she cooks chicken even better than she —'

'I'll have you know Erin did *not* fry that chicken, nor make the salad.'

He affected an expression of stunned disbelief. He even rolled his eyes in mock awe. 'Not *you!* Jackie, don't tell me you cooked all this?'

She glared. 'If I were closer I'd hit you!'

'Why? I'm just amazed. Not only are you beautiful, lovely, madly desirable, exquisite by starlight, golden by sunlight — but damned if you can't also cook. It's just too much.'

She laughed. 'Don't stop now. You were doing very well for a moment there.'

He grinned, bit down upon the drumstick and kept watching her. It was the truth. She actually *was* exquisite and golden.

Overhead, a shiny black crow landed in a treetop, cocked a greedy eye at the food and began a great clamour. He was shortly joined by two other crows, and that was a bit much.

Fred reached for a stone. He didn't find one but the crows were old and wily. They took the hint and went flapping away screaming what had to be crow-imprecations, back.

Fred noticed that Jacqueline was toying with her food, not eating it. He said something and her lovely, steely eyes lifted to his face. 'It won't go down,' she said. 'I'm ashamed of not being hungry. Usually, after a ride, I eat like a horse.'

He nodded. 'You are in love. That's a symptom. I read in a magazine one time that people in love lose their appetites.'

She watched him lick his fingers and reach for another piece of fried chicken, and scowled at him. 'Then you haven't been telling me the truth, Fred Nufall. You're eating like a —'

'Wait. That isn't true with men. At least not with this one. You see, my sweet, the more in love I become with you, the hungrier I become. By next summer I'll probably weigh three hundred and fifty pounds.'

'Oh no you won't. You've got a beautiful physique and you're going to keep it if I have to put you on a diet.'

'Bossy women; kiss them, whisper in their ear, and right away they get bossy.'

He wiped his fingers on a checkered gingham napkin, slowly turned to move over beside her, and by the time she caught the glitter in his eye it was too late. He had reached her, had one of her hands in his grip, and although she could have wrenched free she did not make the effort. She let him ease her back upon the grass, watched his thick shoulders blot out the light, and raised upwards to meet his lips.

They lay silent for a moment afterwards, then she ran fingers through his hair. 'I never would have believed it, Fred. I'd have thought it possible that I could find what I was — blindly — searching for, out here at my grandfather's place.'

'Are you sure you have?' he murmured, and kissed her throat.

'I'm sure.'

'You weren't so sure a couple of days ago.'

'A couple of centuries ago, love. Why is it people measure time by things like days and weeks and months and years. Time is something inside you that can stand entirely still, suspended, for long periods of time. Or like now it can be so fleet you don't realize how much of it has passed.'

He reared up to look down into her exquisite face. 'Does chicken and potato salad always affect you this way?'

She raised a hand as though to slap him, then gently put it to his cheek and it was cool to him, cool and soft.

'Not chicken,' she retorted. 'Love. And that reminds me.'

Whatever it reminded her of she got no chance to enunciate. He dropped down and kissed her again, moving his lips across her mouth until her arms came up to hold him still closer.

Somewhere just beyond sight that raffish old sly crow was back scolding in his same raucous voice again, but the two people down below didn't even hear him.